To Katrina,

    Love From,

Charlotte

    2007 Christmas

The Gift of Christmas

OTHER BOOKS BY NELLIE P. STROWBRIDGE

Far From Home: Dr. Grenfell's Little Orphan

Doors Held Ajar (tri-author)

Dancing on Ochre Sands

Shadows of the Heart

Widdershins

The Gift of Christmas

NELLIE P. STROWBRIDGE

FLANKER PRESS LTD.
ST. JOHN'S, NEWFOUNDLAND
2006

Library and Archives Canada Cataloguing in Publication

Strowbridge, Nellie P., 1947-
  The gift of Christmas / Nellie P. Strowbridge.

ISBN 1-894463-94-3

  1. Christmas. I. Title.

GT4985.S79 2006   394.2663   C2006-905200-X

PRINTED IN CANADA

FLANKER PRESS
ST. JOHN'S, NL, CANADA
TOLL FREE: 1-866-739-4420
WWW.FLANKERPRESS.COM

First Canadian edition printed September 2006

10 9 8 7 6 5 4 3 2 1

We acknowledge the financial support of: the Government of Canada through the Book Publishing Industry Development Program (BPIDP); the Canada Council for the Arts which last year invested $20.0 million in writing and publishing throughout Canada; the Government of Newfoundland and Labrador, Department of Tourism, Culture and Recreation.

To Clarence, who has given me gifts of faith, hope, love, and generosity of spirit during the thirty-five years of our marriage. Also to my parents, George Clayton Kennedy (1923–2006) and Lillian Maud Upshall, who gave Christmas from a puncheon full of love.

CONTENTS

At any other time of the year, we end a phone conversation with goodbye and cut a connection. At Christmastime we end a conversation with Merry Christmas and make a connection.

Making And Keeping Memories

When we go home to the past, Christmas becomes the warm rock in the bed of a long, chilly winter; when we come home to the present, Christmas creates a patchwork quilt of many Christmases.

The Yuletide Card

Few people bless the fellow who created the first Christmas card. Some even wish he'd been hanged with his yuletide greeting. The very late M.C.T. Dobson, the Christmas card instigator, lies peacefully unaware of rumblings in the heads of dissenters. In all fairness to him, he sent only the first card. Sir Henry Cole, in cahoots with J.C. Horsley, produced the first commercial card in 1846. Temperance groups denounced the card showing a family group whose centre members were having a cup of cheer. Nevertheless, Tucks, the art printers, began printing the card in the 1870s.

Christmas enveloping goes back three years before Christmas cards. In 1840, Richard Doyle sent his message to his friends in a hand-decorated folder. Soon Christmas messages were being sent for a penny. Perhaps that's where "A penny for your thoughts" came from.

Nevertheless, there will always be someone to complain about the cost of Christmas cards. One old renegade, who is probably cut from the same genetic cloth as Ebby Scrooge, grumbles: "I minds the time the dang things took two cents to mail."

Mary Dorman Lardie, Hallmark Cards's first official staff writer, penned her favourite Christmas message during the Depression. She wrote: "Although it's just a ten-cent card / Please don't put up a holler / I know you're worth a dollar card / But I ain't got a dollar."

In 1977, Hallmark created a card depicting "Three Little Angels." It became America's bestselling Christmas card, netting twenty-three million dollars. The card shows three angels wearing halos, with their hands together in prayer. Michelle Keller, a spokeswoman for Hallmark, credited its cuteness and religious sentiment for its popularity.

During post-Confederation, dollar(s) cards came into vogue. They were like today's cards: big, small, colourful, well-versed, inspirational, secular, humorous, upbeat, and offbeat. Some were puffed-up and perfumed. There were cards with lace bells, satin wreaths, red velvet bows, and rhinestoned trees that twinkled like stars. One type of card had Santa, with an angel's hair beard, wiggling against the sponge gluing him to the card. When I was a 1960s teenager, I sacrificed a stuffed card to my curiosity. I emptied its anemic powder and used it as face powder for a Mary, Queen of Scots look.

These days, Christmas cards appear in our mailboxes during the first week in December: cards artistically created, and poetically written, and ordinary cards with beautiful verses, and beautiful cards with mediocre verses. They come less garnished than they did when I was growing up. But they sometimes come, opening to the music of a Christmas carol.

When cards begin to arrive, I string three red cords across the mantel above the fireplace in hopes that they will soon be full. By Christmas Eve, cards are overlapping each other. The cards take us on a journey to Bethlehem and to the humble and mystical presence of the Christ Child born to stable-bound Mary and Joseph, to the shepherds and their heavenly sightings, and from there to the kings from the East bearing gifts.

Religious scenes shift to cards showing the nostalgic age of horse-drawn carriages bearing gentlemen in high hats and ladies in billowing Scarlet O'Hara finery. There are peaked, red-roofed houses in settings of pure-spun snow on some cards, and on others a lit or unlit fireplace with stockings hung. On another card is Old Saint Nick, an identified flying object coming to paint the season red.

Diverse Christmas cards greet individuals who come together for a brief connection during this holy and secular season. Sometimes a Hanukkah card gets slipped in among Christmas cards, reminding Christians of their Jewish heritage.

When I was growing up, Christmas cards spanned the geographical distance that separated my family from relatives and friends. A faraway look would come into my mother's eyes as she remembered Selma, an old buddy of hers, when they were both "in service" in St. John's during the war years.

V e would laugh at unfamiliar names like Phonse, Uncle Pleb, and Heed. It was Edith (Heed), my uncle Charles's wife, who cut off my mother's black ringlets when she was a little girl. Then there was old Sol. He could spin a spell, break a spell, or reverse a curse.

There were cards that came with a familiar first name and an unfamiliar last name. There must have been a lot of young people who grew up, got married, and used my mother – their aunt, godmother, or cousin – to begin a Christmas card list. Sometimes there was no return address. Mom would mull over cards from people whose names she couldn't place. Some cards would become perennials with no return address – like Susie's. Finally Susie didn't send a card, and Mom knew something had happened to her.

What is as rewarding as getting and sending cards is keeping them year after year. Those of us who like to keep cards can go back to Christmases past by looking at them. Some cards hold pictures of a new addition to a family, letters containing highlights of the year past, or just a note jotted inside. My cousin, Ruby, and my brother-in-law, Bill, take time to give a report of the year past: highlights and struggles.

Today I look at cards from people no longer alive, and it's as if these people are lifted from the fog of forgetfulness and dropped into my thoughts. My aunt Mary, who had grey curls and a sweet smile, died when she was a little younger than I am now. That she existed is reaffirmed and hung like a Christmas ornament on my tree of memories.

Forgotten people suddenly traipse through memory in a card. There's the newlyweds who want to begin the family tradition. Some couples want to show off a new gift: their first-born, or a first school picture. There's a daughter's old boyfriend's mother who wants to keep in touch.

I look through old cards and I think, *Everything we ever needed that mattered is wished for us inside these cards, either in a verse or in the sender's handwriting.* A friend scribbles on one Christmas card, "Thanks for your thoughts."

My thoughts were borne inside a Christmas card after her newborn Christmas gift was given and taken on the same day. Another writes, "If you see so-and-so, say hello." That's what I call extended greetings.

The year Canadians got a postal code, Uncle Si would get red in the face trying to figure out how to tick it off on the preprinted box on the Christmas envelope. Once done, he could mail a card for twenty-nine cents instead of thirty-four cents. Still, today's Christmas card is not very costly, considering the price of other gifts. A card draws us inside the warmth of another's thoughts. When we receive a card, we are the recipient of a thought, worth much more than a stamp. It is a gift – a gift of remembrance.

By buying charity cards to give to friends and relatives, we can also bring a gift of hope to those whose lives are at risk. The money provides clean water, nutrition, health care, education, and sanitation to children in more than a hundred developing countries.

Christmas bursts out in colour and poetry as we gather all the expressions of faith, hope, and charity – gifts we want for ourselves – and hand them to others, sometimes, in the best way we know how. In a Christmas card.

Marcus Bach, writing in *Unity*, said it well: "Christmas cards . . . represent something deep and beautiful in the human spirit when procrastination and the swift passage of time have severed precious ties. They are passports voluntarily renewed by the spirit of the season. No apologies needed. No excuses necessary. No explanations called for. It is Christmas."

Let's Go Skeetin'

Long before Mr. Winkle got on skates, many people did some form of skating, though not for exercise or sport. Back in the bone age of skating, people attached shanks or ribs of animals to their boots with thongs to help them move fast over the frozen ponds that separated their meeting places. Then came the iron blade and, finally, by the nineteenth century, the all-steel blade came into use.

I was lucky to have been born at the right time and in the right place to take in winter's magical sport. The undulating water in the pond beside my door served as a swimming pool during the summer. By Christmas, it was breathed on by Jack Frost, until a magnificent silent spread was laid, and fastened to the shore.

Mother Nature handed me the opportunity to "go skeetin'" on a silver platter. Sometimes it was silver; other times it froze crystal clear. Often I lay on the ice and put my hooded head against its glacial body to listen to deep rumblings in its belly. Looking as if they were caught under glass, strawlike bulrushes sprawled, and beaver mores waited for spring to resurrect its lilies.

Once the skating season began, the big basement door of our house was often opened and banged shut as children from the cove came inside to put on their skates. They left their boots behind until they came back, shouting and laughing about the good time they had skeetin'. They stayed in the basement long enough to get warm before they headed home.

The first Christmas that I received a brand-new pair of white ice skates, I was delirious with joy at the sight of the pond framed in the kitchen window. It had solidified overnight into a stretch of shining, mysterious black marble. There was not even a sprinkle of snow. I gazed in awe, holding my breath. My feet, tired of clunking in heavy boots through mud or snow, were itching to slip into skates, their shiny, sharp blades lifting, twirling, and writing in carefree movement on the pond's magical blackboard.

Alas, it was Sunday, a day not to be indulged in by doing something as frivolous as skating. Adults told me I should be glad I got a gift when it wasn't *my* birthday. The least I could do on Jesus's birthday was to make room for Him in the inn of my heart, and while I was at it, pray for sinners who wouldn't let Him into theirs. Some of these were on their way to hell, even as we spoke. I was sure these bad people would rather be on ice. Maybe I should pray for them to get a pair of skates. A person couldn't do anything bad enough to go to hell while skating. Cove bullies should have had skates. They satisfied their envy by making snowballs with a rock inside each ball. They used the snowballs to hit moving, live targets, like skaters' behinds. Other children who didn't have skates buckled Carnation milk cans under their boots and "canned" their way across the ice.

Lucky for me, Boxing Day came with the same climate as Christmas. My new skates cut abstract art on the pond's frozen pane, shaving crystal-clear ice into white flakes. By evening, stars twinkled high overhead and the moon shone a silver spotlight over a plate, black like the night, beneath my feet, as I arched into the air, arms flung out, almost weightless. The pond soon came alive with dark figures, and their shadows, moving across it, guys and girls paired off, their skates scratching the ice. Cracking sounds echoed through the sharp air. It was the closest I came to dancing.

Mother Nature's temperament was always reflected in the pond's colours and texture. After a rainfall, a new layer of water often froze, holding patterns of footprints, sled runners, and even vehicle tracks from trucks and cars racing over its surface, oblivious to thunderous booms travelling underneath. After a tumble of snow, light at first, then heavy, and a wind as sharp as any skate, swirling it, the pond was a spoiled rink. Once rain fell, Jack Frost turned it into a frozen snotty crust that I often risked skating over to find smooth spots. Often I landed on my face on needles of ice.

Sometimes the weather turned mild, and rain beat against the pond and stopped only when it had left an inch of water.

I would don my skates and sail through the puddled surface, so calm it held the reflection of the snow-patched hills and the blue sky under my feet. Heaven and earth became one scene, and I was the wind rippling it. Sometimes I fell. Then I hurried home, exhilarated but shivering. My drenched jacket and leggings were soon hung behind the kitchen stove that gave off enough heat to toast them. My wet cuffs were left to dry in the "warmer" above the stove.

All was not lost with a heavy snowfall. Hills cradling the pond were borrowed by adventurous sled riders who climbed them, smoking the air with hot breaths. For me, the thrill began with my bottom on a little red sled making a steep, breathtaking descent down the hills and across the pond, using ice stabbers to hurry me along.

Still, the biggest thrill of all was the sight of a skater's perfect plateau, and the echo of children's voices: "Let's go skeetin'."

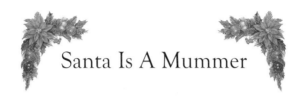

Santa Is A Mummer

"Peel'd, patched and piebald,
linseywoolsey brothers.
Grave mummers? Sleeveless some,
and shirtless others."

So wrote Alexander Pope (Dunciad III, 115). He was talking about mummers who roamed Ireland and England long before mummers – or jannies – hit the Rock of Newfoundland.

No one seems to know if mummer is the nickname for janny, or if it's the other way around. "Depends on which part yer frum," would squeak one mummer – or janny.

Despite the Newfoundland Legislative Assembly passing an Act on June 25, 1861, making it illegal for any person in Newfoundland to publicly wear a mask or disguise, unless licenced by a magistrate, mummering continued.

During a spell when Newfoundlanders were trying to discard the traditional mummer's mould, old duds were discarded, along with peaky-roofed houses and attics that stored old clothes. Living rooms were carpeted and kitchens got floor coverings that mummers wouldn't dare wet. You could no longer encounter a mummer rolling on canvas floors, mopping up the dirty puddles he'd made. The mummer was now "clothed properly and in his right mind."

Mummers might have gone from being a distinct breed to becoming an extinct breed had the cultural renaissance not overtaken some of us. C.F.A.'s (Come-from-aways) were tickled by what they perceived to be our unique character. They latched on to the Rock like barnacles. All the better to write about us. Preserving the difference became fashionable.

Newfoundlandia took hold, and foolhardy folk found rummage clothes in Grandma's closet, and set out to twitch the nostalgic nerve buried in the Newfoundland soul. They entered through the eyeballs, nostrils, and earholes of those who wanted to nurse the good old days.

Perhaps there comes a time in all our lives (a sign of aging) when we want to do something as foolish as dress up in old duds and act someone else's age. It's easy to get invited into homes. There are still brave souls who believe that anyone who comes to their door at Christmastime, even if he is masked and menacing-looking, has a janny good reason for doing so. He is automatically invited inside.

My mummering friends and I once (or twice) decided to go to the homes of people we knew. One of us planned to unmask and vouch for the rest.

That wasn't necessary. Our head mummer, standing outside the door with a hump on his back and a lump on his belly, knew the tricks of his trade. He rang the doorbell, then leaned against the door. When it was opened he fell in.

What was the host to do? He drew back with the kind of confounded look a victim of *Candid Camera* might wear when he knows something strange is happening but doesn't want to make a fool of himself by reacting. The creature passing him, and going up the stairs in a half-dance, with his bumps shaking and his Jew's harp making screeching noises, was obviously someone he knew. The lumps behind him were also people he knew. Who else would be so brazen? The host looked toward his living room, where a party was in progress. Here was his entertainment for the evening – mummers from heaven.

I tossed back the chain skivering the side of my panty-hosed face (more panty than hose), kicked off my vamp-encased boots, and shimmied up the stairs. Someone saw my tam with its butterfly brooch and called out, "The Wonderful Grand Band must have turned Nanny Hynes loose. Her face looks kinda squished, though."

Wearing red gloves outlined in large white stitching that an aunt had bought at a flea market, I tried to straighten my face and push my mouth back in place. After all, you can help the face you weren't born with.

"What's ya got on at all," someone said with a shake of his head.

Wrapping my lips around my teeth, I squeaked, "I had me nightcap on an' me stockin's stuffed wit' me feet when a knock come on der windar and a voice called: 'Hark! Dere's a pardy on der go.' I grabbed me shawl an' tied me hot water bottle 'round me middle ter keep der drafts out, and 'ere I is wit' me timepiece. When it alarms everyone, it'll be time fer me ter git hop and go 'ome. 'Ere, 'ave a pickled sweet. I put some pickles an' sweets in me purse last Christmas an' forget 'em. Don't everyone come at wunce," I cautioned.

They didn't!

"What will it be to drink?" asked the hostess.

"I'n gonna 'ave a glass of swanky to go wit' a chaw on der 'ardtack I got in me pocket. I don't need a straw. I got a licorice in me purse to give some flavour to me drink. 'Tis rite 'ere stickin' out 'round der clamp on me purse."

The partygoers looked at the gatecrashers and had a good laugh. One pretended to know us. "Wearing that face doesn't alter you a bit," he taunted. Our stickup mummer stuck his stick in the air, and the bold fellow covered his nose rather than risk having it sideswiped.

One curious guest asked the mummer who looked like someone from *Planet of the Apes*, "Weird yer come frum, me son?"

The mummer sighed. "I live so far away that I have to pass the moon on the way here. When I passed this rock before, it was only a speck in the Atlantic. It's grown some."

The last time the fellow had gone mummering, he'd

looked like Madame Butterfly. He was taken to the hospital with symptoms of a heart attack that ended up being an acute attack of indigestion, which became a cute incident after all, as he tried to explain why he was wearing lipstick next to his moustache. Mummering is one of the few times men get to wear lipstick, red nail polish, girdles, and garner a smile from women for doing it.

"Got your accordion for a jig?" asked the host.

"No accardin," squeaked the mummer in the underwear jeans. "I got me hook-and-line to jig a fish, though der ones in dat aquarium don't look much for size. I better git goin'." The cord of his chainsaw was tied around one foot. He pulled hard on it, trying to start up his rubber boot. Suddenly, he went hopping around the room, complaining that he had no brakes, no steering, and no switchoff button. Somebody yelled: "Watch out!" just before he was stopped by a foot that sent him into the lap of a startled guest.

We visited ten homes, getting inside all of them without a hitch. One of us got laughed at for jumping around like a chair on two legs, while another was accused of whistling backwards. There was a lot of bold talk from people to mummers in no hurry to show their faces. When all was said and done, some foolish and otherwise, and the clock alarmed, we got up and went home.

Christmas Homecoming

A few days before the Christmas week of 1964, the "Newfie Bullet" chugged its way up snow-capped hills and snaked through the white valleys of Newfoundland. It picked up Betty, my sister, who was on her Christmas break from teaching high school in Springdale. Then the eastbound train journeyed on to Windsor, where I had gone to finish my last year in school. I waited eagerly for the train to take me to Whitbourne, where my father would be waiting in his truck. Betty and I were going home to Hibb's Cove for Christmas. Perched on the rugged east coast, Hibb's Cove is one of Newfoundland's oldest fishing settlements.

Betty was waving at me from the train window as it pulled into Windsor Station. As usual, my striking older sister was dressed in an outfit she had designed, looking composed except for her eyes. They were clouded.

"I have something to tell you," she said quietly.

She said this while I was still puffing and blowing after dragging my bags through bitter wind and blinding sheets of snow to clamber aboard the train.

"I can't tell you until the train goes," she added in a serious tone.

She paused and I gulped. "Tell me what? What's wrong?"

"Mom said not to tell you until you were on the train – a moving train."

I sighed in relief. At least Mom was all right.

"Why didn't she want me to know *whatever* until I was on the train?" I asked apprehensively.

"In case you wouldn't come home for Christmas."

Not come home? Christmas wouldn't be Christmas without going home to Hibb's Cove, where dark snow-caked cliffs rose about the sea and wound their way up over the hills to the house where I was born. The house sat beside a pond framed in our kitchen window to which the four seasons gave a thousand faces. Home was where my stockingful of Christmas memories lay. I had never *not* been home for Christmas. What kind of calamity could keep me from coming home this year?

Suddenly the train jerked, sputtered, and began to move.

"I can tell you now," Betty announced, fingering the winter fur on her wool suit.

"Well, there's still a chance I could jump off. The train isn't going very fast and I could land in a snowbank," I said, miffed and tense at the same time. "I don't know how Mom could think I wouldn't come home," I added.

"Well, because –" Betty's look got uncomfortable. Then she blurted, "I think eight is enough in a family, too."

"So Mom is going to have another baby?" I said flatly, not thrilled but relieved that no one had died.

"In February." My sister's eyes turned to the window. Snow-laden trees appeared to be racing past us. "Mom thinks this will spoil your holidays. She knows how much you love Christmas."

"Spoil my Christmas? What about hers?"

Suddenly the scene of my leave-taking four months before came back vividly. Mom had cried when I left. I had promised to be home for Christmas. Something had crossed my mind even then, but the image of my mother's middle looking more rounded had been so swift I hadn't thought about it since. She was not one to show emotion, and I had wondered why she was crying simply because I was going away. There were still five children at home to keep her company.

By the time we reached home, the sun was shining on glittering snow. A recent rain had melted the snow on the pond, which had then frozen and left the water looking like black glass – a skater's dream that made my feet itch. When I opened the porch door and went into the kitchen, my mother was nowhere in sight. I hurried through the long hall to the front porch where the Christmas goodies waited. I glanced at the front room, where the decorated tree always stood. It would be a perfect tree. My father made sure of that every Christmas Eve. Multicoloured lights always shimmered through the magical night of rustling paper. Carefully wrapped presents would be spread out from underneath.

But there was one present that wouldn't be opened until

February. I felt anxious, hoping that gift would not threaten the life of my mother.

I felt an urgency to get to her room. I knocked, then gently pushed open the door. As I did, I saw my mother crying quietly, her back to me. Her dark hair, covered in a hairnet, lay rolled on the nape of her neck. The strings of her flowered apron were tied at the back in a knot instead of in a bow, because of her swollen body. I felt a gush of tearful emotion. My mother, usually so steady, seemed to be caught in emotional turmoil.

I rushed in and put my arms around her, my glance dropping to her enlarged front, but not letting it come between us. I kissed her tear-stained cheek and said gently, "Merry Christmas, Mom."

"I thought your Christmas would be spoiled," she whispered.

"I don't know why you would think that," I answered lightly.

She had underestimated the love of a daughter, and the power of Christmas in her heart. It was true, I was afraid for my mother to have another baby. But Christmas celebrates life and gives us faith for our journey into the unknown. I had seen her go through a life-threatening pregnancy before, and it would happen again when my youngest sister, Carolann, was born, with eyes so incredibly blue an angel must have snatched the colour from a lit Christmas bulb.

Coming home for Christmas is more than a tangible journey. We often come home to a place in our hearts where we have never been before – a place of peace through acceptance. It is a place where we all belong.

Old Christmas Day

When I lived in Ontario, I felt cheated out of Old Christmas Day. "What's with all the Christmas trees gone bare?" I asked my Toronto friend on Boxing Day. Here I was, finally ready to relax and enjoy the Twelve Days of Christmas, and lo and behold, what did I see as I peered out my window on the day after Christmas, but trees that had put a shine in the eyes of children and adults with their bright dress-up, all stripped and laid out on the cold, white sidewalks for their funeral at the garbage dump or recycling bins. Wasn't that sacri-Christmas?

It's comforting to know that won't happen here in Newfoundland. We savour the days following Christmas Day. The shopping is done, the Christmas wrappings undone, and the ritual of binding family ties continues in the enjoyment of the Twelve Days of Christmas. This is the time to visit friends and go on a janny jaunt, even if mummering has lost its significant place in Newfoundland traditions.

I, along with many other Newfoundlanders, resist a cold turkey quick slide into January bleakness. We like to wean ourselves from the season's enchanting presence. Tree lights are turned on less often.

Newfoundlanders keep Christmas until Old Christmas Day. By then the tree's head is bowed, the branches have lost their perkiness, and needles, dry enough to draw blood, start leaving the tree for a nice place to sink themselves into, namely our bare feet. Finally, the tree is lowered and its trunk is readied to give its last flare from the fireplace.

On the Twelfth Day of Christmas, we reluctantly leave the bright glow of Christmas, with its fleeting wonders, and give the season its last rites, storing another memory ornament of Christmases past.

Mummering's The Word

Many people believe that all Newfoundlanders have either gone mummering or have had mummers in. Some have done both at some time in their lives.

Until recently, I had done neither. This may have been because I grew up in a Missioner's family – Pentecostal, today – where it was believed that anyone who dressed in Biblical getups was making fun of the wise men, as if they cared. Sometimes I would watch through the window of our living room as mummers, bent against the wind, made their way through sweeping snow. Some of them would thump against our door only to be turned away. Others would pass on by. My parents did not know that mummering began in England with "St. George and the Dragon" – an allegorical expression of the triumph of good over evil.

A few days before Christmas one year, I confessed to a cousin that I would like to go mummering before the custom got mummified. Cousin, who can become very energetic at short notice, sprang from her chair. It took her almost a day to round up some gear and some other mummers. Neither is on standby, as in years past. Cousin enlisted a daughter, a son-in-law, and a veteran mother-in-law I'll call Jess. She loved mummering and considered it her Christmas marm-about (get-out). It didn't take her long to find some old duds, including an arse bag (loose underwear) to go over her trousers. I got rigged in hubby's old clothes and drew a moustache where I hoped none would ever grow. In the old days, moustaches and eyebrows were made from maldow, the green, hairlike moss on dead tree branches, giving the mummers a hoary look. Cousin took one look at me and said I was supposed to go faceless, like Gouzenko. She then draped a piece of muslin over my head and cut holes for my eyes and nose. The cloth was tucked inside my collar, and an old hat was pressed on my head.

There was little chance of anyone recognizing me, anyway. I lived in a community where neighbours could be strangers, unlike yesteryears when people would recognize mummers by an article of clothing, or even by the stitch work of the women in the community. Sharp-eyed residents might be able to unmask someone's Uncle John simply by the way he had cleaved the split he was using to tap on doors as he went from house to house. With mummering activities strung from Christmas Eve to Twelfth Night, it took a lot of digging in attic trunks to get enough clothes to keep the neighbours guessing.

When we drove up to Old Jess's place and honked the

horn, she limped out of the house thumping the ground with a stick. She climbed into the car and poked me in the ribs. Old Jess was wearing a ski mask over her blackened face. When she laughed I saw her teeth encased in foil wrap. Twenty Christmases ago, a gap in her teeth had given her away. She had taken no chances since. People who knew what she was up to nicknamed her "Foiled Jess" behind her back, and they let her pass as if they didn't know her.

Cousin decided we would only go to the homes of people who had put out the welcome mat for mummers.

"My dear," said Old Jess to the little girl who answered the thump of her stick on the first door, "do you believe in ghosts?"

The little girl hesitated. Then she answered timidly, "Only the Holy Ghost." Then, with Old Jess's belly laugh clapping her ears, she darted inside.

Old Jess stomped into the porch and tapped her stick on the canvas floor. She wiped her boots on a plaited mat and called in a high-pitched voice, "Any mummers in der night?"

A middle-aged woman appeared, wiping her hands on a bibbed apron, and, without any show of surprise, invited us in. As I stooped to remove my boots, she said, "Never mind your boots; you can sit in the kitchen." She brought chairs. Then she asked for an "accardin" so we could have a jig.

Old Jess and the man of the house wrapped arms and heaved around the kitchen shaking the floors while our he-mummer stretched the accordion to its limits. Then they sat down and the man tried to guess who we were. Old Jess ignored his attempts by licking her lips and complaining, "I'm as dry as a cork lid. I want something to wet me whistle."

"You'd get nar bit of grog here as long as you got that face on, but, as it happens, I arn't got a leak in the house anyway."

I looked at the ceiling and he laughed, nodding his head toward Old Jess. "I don't know who you got with ya, but it thinks that leaks are only what you get in the roof."

Old Jess knew the people in the next house. We followed her straight into the kitchen with only a quick knock. An elderly couple looked up from the table. The man eyed us keenly and asked, "Where did you stragglers come from? Me and the missus were just mimpsing our cup of tea before turning in for the night."

"Mummersville," Cousin's daughter answered in a squeaky voice.

"I think I knows you," the man said, biting into a cracker. "You're so-and-so's daughter. I forgets his name now."

"You don't know any of us," Old Jess said bluntly. Then she proceeded to ask the man in vulgar terms how he was treating his wife.

When I tried to apologize for her behaviour, the man laughed. "At Christmastime, anyone can say anything they like in this house."

Old Jess got a swig of booze and hot water there. That kept her spirits pumped up for the next house. There she had to bang long and hard before a man came to the door. He turned back to call to his wife, "We got mummers with some nasty-looking faces."

"Bring them in," she called.

We followed him in, only to find ourselves caught in the uneasy eye-lights of strayed mainlanders, who were having their first encounter with mummers. To them, we were masked people holding up the home of a defenceless elderly couple.

"What do you know about mummers?" Old Jess asked, poking her face in front of one startled fellow.

He drew back, hesitating before answering. "I've heard that 'mummers' is a name for bad actors."

"Bad actors," snorted Old Jess. "We're no actors. We're ourselves just cutting loose. We've been called everything from mummers, jannies, ownsooks, morgans, darbies, fools, and a whole lot of other names."

"Now I'll have a beer," Old Jess announced, pulling a straw from her pocket. "Leave it in the can. One year I got short-taken when someone put Epsom salts in me grog."

A large German shepherd came into the room and sniffed us. It started wagging its tail, which tipped Old Jess's beer onto the carpet. She immediately dropped to her knees and wiped it with her gloves. "I'll suck on them later," she explained.

An elderly woman came shuffling into the kitchen muttering, "You should have offered them some of me swanky. I boiled me cranberries a'purpose with lots o' sugar, 'cause I knowed there'd be jannies this year for sure."

"Is it mummering or jannying?" asked one mainlander – now in recovery.

"Mummering's the word," answered Old Jess.

Mum was the word for Old Jess, who wouldn't throw up her false face first nor last.

The snow was falling softly, like in "Silent Night," as we made our way to the car. I was glad I'd gone mummering, and pleased that there were still people in the world who had enough faith and trust in humankind to invite masked strangers into their homes.

Only in Newfoundland.

Christmas Shopping

I don't suppose we will ever know who first complained that Christmas is too commercialized. It couldn't have been the wise men, because they went shopping for expensive gifts before visiting the child in the manger. No matter! It caught on.

Some people would rather have their feet shredded than take them to the shopping malls those last few days before Christmas. They have a very good reason. Christmas is not what we find at the stores. We find people – people who are shopping for Christmas without their Christmas spirits to keep them in line, people complaining about the commercialization of the season. Spurred on by messages coming over the airways, or appearing in newspaper advertisements warning that there are only so many shopping days till Christmas, they go out and deck the malls with their presence, making sure they do everything to keep Christmas as commercialized as their credit cards can make it. After all, it's hard to break with tradition: a time to give other people either the gift that counts, or the thought that counts, sometimes wrapped around a gift that doesn't.

Shoppers tire of running around stores, like animals chasing their tails, while visions of savings, advertised in flyers, dance in their heads, only to be told: "We are out of this – and that." They try to be good for goodness' sake and not say something that would make Rudolph's red nose turn blue. Voices on intercoms drag people toward in-store specials which become more special when there's a stampede of shoppers grabbing at items in a bin and holding on to them for dear life – whether they want them or not, their fingernails like the claws of an alley cat. As one teenaged shopper nursed the claw marks on her hand, she looked mournfully toward the line she'd vacated. It had stretched beyond her patience. Frustrated, she dumped her "specials" and fled from the scene, her tongue and her teeth doing a dance.

Two biddies eyed her, and one commented with a tut-tut: "My dear, the young ones got their belly buttons buttoned with jewellery that's hanging out with the buttons on their jeans. That's the fat ones. The skinny ones got theirs clinging to their backbone for dear life. 'Tis scandalous, sure."

"Yes," the other agreed, "the way of the world today is like nothing we've ever seen."

A checkout queue provides the venue for shoppers to vent. They bash Christmas commercialism and greed while supporting its commercialism and greed. The cost of keeping Christmas has become something every shopper can use to introduce a conversation or as a filler when a conversation with strangers and acquaintances standing side by side or back to front in a checkout line begins to sag.

What we need, and seldom get, is soothing music that will let us slip and slide through the line cushioned by peaceful carols. The rang-a-tang noise of some Christmas music is enough to make a shopper's frazzled nerves leave her body and wrap around a shopper who stands in line describing the night before Christmas that came after a drinking binge.

You get to smile as a silver-haired man in line says to a bald-haired one: "I think I'm paying too much for this Christmas gift." And the other one answers: "Now George – eh, Scrooge – there's no U-Haul behind a hearse."

A woman rushes from the back of the line, explaining to the cashier that she has to get checked out right away. Her husband just died. You see her in the next store and wonder if she decided to wait for her husband to cool before she goes home.

It's terrible what Christmas shopping can do to sweet, accommodating old ladies. I was standing behind one granny who looked like she could knit a sweater with a turn of her hand, or whip up a meal faster than you could say grace. Here she was shaking the grey bun perched on the back of her head, up and down and sideways. I could tell by the look on her face she wasn't exercising a stiff neck. Her eyes were almost beating themselves against her bifocals as they flashed angry signals. She mumbled about the red-cheeked cashier, who was casually tearing pieces of price tags off articles of clothes, as if she had lead in her fingers.

Granny almost took my eye out with the corner of the red dustpan she was carrying when a shopper tried to squeeze in ahead of her. I could understand her agitation. Jumping queues is an addiction for some shoppers. You can never judge a line by its numbers. You could be standing in line behind a shopper who has eight items in an eight-item checkout lane, when along comes another shopper and stands beside the person ahead of you, doubling the items. In response to a frown that might tighten your lips, the line crasher is generous enough to explain: "I'm not trying to cut in ahead of you, or anything, love." She nods toward the person ahead of you. "We're together, you know."

Only Siamese twins should try that stunt.

It was Granny's fault that I switched lines. Just as I had pulled up behind a line looking equally long to the one Granny was in, she had nodded at me and said, in a loud voice, that the cashier at that checkout was too "stun" for anything. Hoping no one heard her un-Christmasy remarks, but being an impatient shopper, I slipped into Granny's line. She kept monitoring the four lines that were open and grunting when another line moved faster than hers, all the while breathing in my face and blowing her nose whenever the occasion demanded it. Then she'd stick her Kleenex under her tam. "Holes in my pockets," she explained.

If Granny wasn't careful, she could get run over by an unreined *dear*.

I was distracted by a searing pain in the calf of my leg. I turned to find a toddler fastened to me like a leech. He let go and looked up at me, drooling happily. What ever would he want for Christmas! He already had his two front teeth and a taste for blood. His mother grabbed him up and these little teeth ended up puncturing the roll of Christmas paper she was carrying under her arm. She seemed to have more to worry about than whether her child was ingesting lead and other toxic metals from the gift wrap.

A queue can be unpleasant where there are customers with sweaty lips, dripping underarms, and babies bouncing off their shoulders. No one should take hair on a Christmas shopping trip unless it's under cover or fastened to something not living. A fistful of my hair! That's what one baby wanted for Christmas. Men who have been fertilizing their last few strands of hair in the hope that they'll be there at Christmas aren't pleased to have them clutched between the fingers of a young sniper, especially one with a full head of hair. The grandfather behind me had only a ring of hair around his rosy skull. He needed lots of hair to protect his scalp from the batter of a rattle. "Don't, Charlie," a woman said in such a mild voice that Charlie probably thought she was planting another endearment on his cherub ears.

"Come on, Mommy," one boy urged, pulling on a weary shopper's arm, "let Santa bring Auntie a present."

Humbug, said Scrooge about Christmas.

"Humbug," mumbled a man whose wife was wandering

around stores looking for a gift for *his* mother. He slouched bleak-eyed and stunned against a wall, while she wished she could stuff a humbug candy inside humbugger's jaws to sweeten him up a bit.

These days, most of my Christmas gifts are packaged in closets long before the "only so many days before Christmas" countdown. I can wander (or not) as cool as an ice cube through stores, wiggling my toes to jingle bell music while absorbing the sights and sounds of our newly decorated season.

A Christmas Sign

It was a Christmas night. I awoke about four in the morning to see a glow. I blinked a few times before I realized that the warm, glowing light was from an electric candle I had set on my desk by the living room window. I knew I had turned it off early before I went to bed so I could read awhile. If I had not turned it off, the other half would have noticed it when he came to bed a little later.

I got up and went out to turn off the light, not even wondering how it came to be on.

A few days later, a knock came on the door. A man cleared his throat and confessed, with some difficulty, that he had lost his wife in an accident just before Christmas and he felt as if there was no light left in his life or in his heart. On Christmas night, he had left a friend's home where there was laughter and joy and gone home to an empty house and an empty bed. He couldn't sleep, so he had gotten up before dawn and gone for a walk. All the lights had been turned off, and homes and lawns were in darkness. He was trudging along Church

Street, lit only by a street light here and there. His pain was hard, and he wondered how he could go on living in the darkness and loneliness of his loss.

"I passed your house," he said, "and saw a light. I stopped and stared at it. It was drawing me in as if it had healing powers. Minutes later, when I looked back, the light was gone. I see it as a sign now."

I did not tell him that I had plugged the light into an extension cord and I must not have completely disconnected it. Still, what made the connection at that time? There had not been any movement. And why, just in time for a man to find hope? My timing was perfect. Why had the faint glow awakened me in time to disconnect the light so that a man could look behind him and see that it was gone, and believe it was meant for him?

It was for one man, a Christmas light that gave him a sign of hope.

Surviving Christmas
In One Piece Or More

I carried two gifts all through Christmas. One was opened January 25, 1974 and the other was opened January 21, 1978. These two gifts have been the source of many Christmas moments. Through the gift of memory, I open the gift of their childhood again and again.

Last year there was a tall, thin Mrs. Claus at the site of Santa's ice castle in one of the malls. Rosy round cheeks gave her a pleasant look. Wire spectacles pinched the tip of her nose and in the nape of her neck was a neat little bun. She was wearing a long red dress trimmed with a white apron. Janalee asked if this was Little Red Riding Hood's grandmother.

This year, as I tie bows on my mail-away gifts, she asks if there is a real Mrs. Santa Claus.

"Yes, Virginia, there is," I answer playfully.

"I'm not Virginia," she retorts.

"Come to think of it, you're not," I answer, "but asking if

there is a real Mrs. Claus is like asking if God has a wife. Only atheists know for sure."

"What are they?" she asks, perching on my knee.

"Oh, just people who don't believe in God or Santa Claus."

"They won't get to Heaven, then, will they?"

"Well, let's just say that God won't be expecting them."

She's content with that explanation; I don't know if God is. Then she goes on to her favourite question. "How long is it before Christmas gets here?"

"I answered that question last year," I remind her, "and the answer is still the same. It's a long time if you think about it too much and a short time if you don't." I sigh, thinking, *Father Time is a maddening old fellow. He lets time slip tantalizingly slow from his hands, but in his lingering hold is created the exciting prelude to Christmas.*

Janalee dances around, questions tumbling from her lips. I shoo her away.

"Mommy, have you got the Christmas Spirit?" she asks one night as I tuck her into bed.

"Does it dance and wiggle?" I ask playfully.

"Oh Mom," she says in exasperation. "That's a commercial on TV. For worms, I think." She wiggles her nose in disgust.

Christmas is getting too close for comfort, and I solicit my other half to help address some Christmas cards.

He picks one up, scrutinizes it, and gets frivolous. "This card has an anemic-looking mother on it, and she isn't wearing a wedding ring. The nude kid on her lap is about ten pounds overweight, and there he is holding onto an apple as if he can't wait to say grace before he eats it. Both of them have rings around their heads – a sure sign of bad weather – or, in this case, a bad Christmas for whoever you mail these cards to."

I lift my pen from addressing the cards and fix him with a steely eye. "That fat baby and his anemic-looking mother are *waiting* to be mailed."

"Oh well," he answers, pretending to be meek, "that puts the picture in a different light." He immediately addresses one solitary card.

The next Saturday morning, I'm standing on a chair hanging Christmas cards when three-year-old Michael rushes in wiping his mouth. "Water, Mommy," he croaks. His eyes are bright and wet. He sneezes and keeps on sneezing.

"It's only pepper," Janalee laughs mischievously.

"Pepper!" I scream. "You've given him pepper!" I almost fall off the chair in my scramble to get to the floor.

Her face crumbles into a cry, and then the Christmas lights decorating her happy thoughts go off. She runs to her room, slamming the door on the Christmas Spirit.

A boy calls and identifies himself as my daughter's boyfriend.

"Call back in ten years," I tell him. I make a note to put a package of garlic gum in Janalee's stocking this Christmas – and every Christmas for the next fifteen years.

Janalee is counting the days to Christmas. They fit the fingers on one little hand now. Michael looks at her. His big, brown eyes are like pools of molasses in sunlight: warm and deep and shining.

The tree is decorated, and in the morning there is the patter of little feet. Michael has discovered a new toy. He touches an ornament, then shakes a branch. "I'm making it dance," he tells me happily.

Janalee takes two dollars out of her bank. She returns from the corner store with my gift. She wraps it carefully and hides it under her bed. Later in the morning Michael drops a cup; it breaks. Janalee promises, "It's okay, Mommy. On Christmas morning you'll be glad."

How do I know the gift under her bed is a cup? She dances around me. "Guess, Mommy, what I've got." Her secrets are like popcorn. When the heat is on, they break out in hint-uendos.

In the meantime, there's a hitch on my new Marty Robins Christmas record. There go Michael's dinky cars on a new racetrack.

A few days before Christmas, I promise the family Chinese food for supper. "I'd like a wok," I say to the other half.

He suggests I take a walk to the store, adding that it will do me good.

At the store two clerks discuss someone's misfortune. I hear one say, "She cut her finger. Then she lost the Band-Aid she'd put on it. Then she found it. That was the worst misfortune of all. She found it in the cooked turkey. It must have followed the savory dressing inside."

I make a note not to wear anything that resembles a Band-Aid when I'm dressing a turkey.

I never put any meat in the freezer while it's still alive, so I'm startled when a furry creature rushes past me as I lift the lid to get the turkey. I've heard of putting batteries in the fridge to preserve their nine lives, but I thought that cats were in charge of their own. Scruples will have only one life, if Michael has his way. Soon she is eyeing the tree as if she is trying to find a way to climb it and replace the angel top. Unlike a dog who lifts his leg to a tree, this cat has left number one and number two presents under the tree. We are lucky that our Christmas tree skirt is a plastic tablecloth. The cat is old enough to be some kitty's grandmother; she should be retired from shenanigans. Instead, she sneaks from her bed when all the house is asleep and bangs on tree decorations until they fall. Then she bites them apart. She sniffs the gifts and has a go at shredding their ribbons and bows.

It's three days to Christmas. We visit Aunt Lizzie Smith at the seniors' home, bringing her Christmas goodies of cake and cookies. "Chase me," she tells the kidlings. She means "follow me s-l-o-w-l-y." She starts toward the closet to get her purse and finds a couple of dollars to put into little hands.

Christmas Eve comes, potent in its scents and pocketed with mysteries. Above our house, a star twinkles as if it has travelled through the centuries for this very moment. Along the dark ribbon of street, between decorated houses, on trees and shrubs, bulbs wink under snowflakes in the new fairy-land.

There are seven hours to midnight. Janalee is coming down with the flu. She lies in bed crying. I'm busy and her demands tire me. I go to her; then I leave her crying softly. I feel a vague disturbance as I hurry to help her father wrap gifts, so I go back and sit on her bed. She says her prayers. "Mommy," she whimpers, "ask Jesus to make me better. My nose is all stuffed up."

We close our eyes and, in the darkness, it seems we are throwing a prayer a million miles into the sky. Then I go out, and return with one wrapped gift. "Listen closely," I tell her. The sniffling stops as I turn the present over. "It sounds like a piano," she says, giggling. I let her open it. The flu is forgotten. Being able to make a little girl forget her discomforts is part of the Christmas magic. She settles down to dream away her last night before Christmas.

Michael calls, "Mommy, my tooth aches."

I hurry in and tell him, "The best way to get rid of a toothache is to fill your mouth with cold water."

"Uh?" His upper lip lifts.

"Yes, Uncle Fred told me what his father told him. If you have a toothache, you fill your mouth with water. Then you sit on the stove until the water boils."

His mouth breaks open into a wide grin, "Mommy, that's funny."

He pulls my hand. "I want a Teddy hand." He lifts my hand and cups his face. Then he settles under the bedclothes.

I stay with him a long time, giving him his Teddy hand and watching him drift into sleep while the moon casts a soft, peaceful glow on his bedroom window.

The night hangs like a huge Christmas stocking, swollen with expectancy. Clocks tick, gently gathering up the hours, minutes, seconds, sifting them in Father Time's hourglass. And then it's Christmas morning.

Darkness is still heavy in the air, but I get up anyway. I always get up before the kidlings. That way I don't risk having a child latch on to my eyelid and pry it up, while a pair of wide eyes stare at my eyeball as if it's a foreign object to be poked at. The real reason is that I don't want to sleep away one more minute of Christmas Day.

I tiptoe into Janalee's room. "Merry Christmas," I whisper into her ear. She stirs, but her dreams hold her. I raise my voice. She jumps up rubbing her eyes.

"It's Christmas Day!" She looks at me. Her eyes widen. She jumps out of bed and runs through the long hall toward the tree. She stops. Christmas has seemed so long in coming, it is as if she must go slowly, carefully, and finally let the magic inside her. She picks up her fat stocking. I get Michael's stocking and we go to our bed. The other half stirs, and settles back asleep. Michael's padded feet are heard. He crawls into our bed. Stockings lose their bumps. Now they lie limp and forgotten. Little cheeks bulge with goodies. For the moment, life is a Cracker Jack box of popcorn and Christmas is a prize.

Soon I dash out of bed with the kidlings in tow. I turn on the phonograph and place the record on the turntable. I set the needle down, and music and narration herald "The Coming of Christ."

Each Christmas, the children hear a trumpeting sound and these words: "The land of Israel, a timeless land, where a thousand years are but as yesterday when it is past, and as a watch in the night. This is the Holy Land, where the Word of God was made manifest . . ."

By the time the music and narration get to ". . . and they opened their treasures and presented to Him gifts . . ." the other half has come to full awareness of the day.

The children are soon running to the tree, followed by two adults acting like youngsters.

I watch Janalee's face as she strips shiny paper off her biggest gift. The doll looks pretty inside her glass cage and Janalee marks a moment – I hope – she'll remember as a "best" memory in coming years. Michael opens his Fisher Price camp set. He sees a small plastic car in Janalee's doll set. He goes after it. Janalee is determined to keep it. There is a fierce tug and angry cries shatter the morning peace. Michael wants what's not his and Janalee wants to keep what's hers.

Not even Christmas morning can bring peace on earth and goodwill among children.

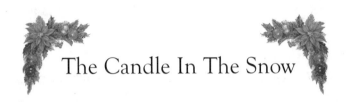

The Candle In The Snow

I had always loved the magical wonder of our fifth season. But since my beautiful young sister died, I found it difficult to believe that no matter what problems we have in life, everything will turn out all right if left in God's hands. I pulled Christmas inside me, as if by doing so I could push out the starkness of her death, and pull in the brightness, pass that "glass darkly" that was between my faith and me. It was as if the perfection of Christmas made pain more glaring – as if God's face was turned toward me, as cold as stone, His silence as dark as the grave. A sliver of bitterness turned inside me.

A fat, red candle surrounded by holly sat on the edge of a shelf in a confectionery store and I bought it. I bought it for her – for her grave on Christmas Eve. I would light it and remember her life rather than her death – if I could. Her hope had been extinguished by an insidious illness. My own faith had become a flickering light, sometimes almost going out in my anger toward God, who made our bodies and allowed them to suffer to the point where some could no longer tolerate the wrenching pain of living.

"Life is beautiful," she wrote in her goodbye note. "Don't you think I want to live?" I remember her, last Christmas alone inside herself, unable to see beauty because of a chemical imbalance. Her death tore away my idealism and optimism. Faith became something I tried to hold like a security blanket, but it was tattered and soiled by my own disillusionment.

It was a bitter cold night on Christmas Eve in 1987 when my family and I visited Nancy's grave. We climbed out of the car and onto a snowbank, hoping it would hold us. The wind was like nails tearing at my face, the cold air stiffening it into a mask. My legs sank through the layers of drifting snow covering the old crust, and I tipped forward and fell face down in the drifts. I pulled my feet up and wiped my face. There was no need to open the heavy iron gate. It couldn't be seen above the deep snow. The cemetery was an icy knob. My husband and children followed me silently. They didn't tell me I was foolhardy – that it was too cold to light a candle on a hill that stands high above the frigid Atlantic Ocean. We struggled to get to the grave, the savage wind clawing at our clothes.

Finally, we made it. My match burst into flame and wavered for a moment before the dark breath of the wind extinguished it. I tried again; the same thing happened. And again. The match's flame lived long enough to touch the candlewick. Just that touch was enough to snuff the delicate flare.

"Let me try," my husband said. A spark of faith stirred inside me. We should be able to light the candle. It was Christmas, a time when childlike faith comes tiptoeing back into our barnacled hearts. Miracles happen! The wind came stronger, grabbing the breath out of our mouths and pressed against our nostrils like some unseen hand. I cupped my hands around the candle. My husband put his hand down in the shelter and lit the match. The flame held, swaying precariously like an acrobat on a tightrope. It touched the candlewick. The wind beat on it, but the match and the candlewick met. The candle took the flame and the match went out.

The candle can't stay lit, I thought. *This manmade candle cannot fight the forces of nature.* Its blue base of flame curved like the bottom of a Christmas bulb, and for a moment it extended up into a yellow flame, shaping itself into a bulb. A tiny speck of warmth stood amidst the vast, cold space around it. It didn't shudder. It danced against the wind, and as the wind swirled around it I held my breath. The wind beat down the flame. Suddenly it rose like a blue butterfly.

I was almost afraid to turn and look as we climbed back over the drifts of snow. As I opened the car door and looked back, I could see the candle's tiny flame reaching up against wind, a light in darkness. All night, the fragile flame was battered by the wind. It would fall, and then rise tall – defiant. It dug a liquid warm pool as its shelter – and lived.

Several people, driving by the cemetery during that long

Christmas night, saw the light of the candle and wondered how it could stay lit. In the morning the candle was out. It had lit the darkness surrounding it, until daylight chased the night from the sky.

The candle had survived obstacles, and had gone out when it had lots of light to give. My sister's light went out when she had lots to give. She did not survive the obstacles that wore her down. But I was still here. I knew she would not want my life to be diminished by her dying. I should be her gentle, loving presence in other people's lives. *I should not become less of a person because of her death,* I thought, as I stood looking at the holly at the base of the candle on that bright, still morning. A death becomes a failure if, out of it, we do nothing but destroy our own hope, faith, and love – and if we do nothing to help others who come after us.

Our lives are candles, flickering and wavering and sometimes holding steady in the adversity of life. We all must hold on, for despite the tragedies that dog our lives, we have much to give.

Christmas teaches us this better than any other season, for Christmas is not just a season. It is a life-holding faith that helps us believe in miracles at times when our lives are clouded by doubts.

An Old-Fashioned Christmas

Christmas was bound to come sooner – not later – whether we were ready or not. The inability to make ready for the perfect Christmas engenders in us the longing for an old-fashioned Christmas, when life was simple and perfect. Mother and Father gave Susie and Joey a gift each – skates or homemade sleds – and they went into winter wonderland with the Christmas Spirit filling every pore.

What ever happened to that perfect world! Admitting it never existed doesn't come easily. Time and nostalgia spin out all the wrinkles and leave wonderful memories of events, gifts, and whiffs of food stirring our senses, bringing back the tangy scent of oranges in tissue paper, and the cold sweetness of apples.

We seem to forget the drawbacks of the old-fashioned Christmas. Many of our forebears might have wanted to be born fifty years after their time if they had known the rich trappings that would come with today's celebrations. They would revel in the wonder of an artificially lit world.

In the olden days, many mothers worked through Christmas while their men celebrated its twelve days by filling their houses with their buddies making merry. The women were expected to stretch their hospitality to the limit by mopping up puddles left by the men's feet, while the men stretched on daybeds to sleep off the spirits from bottles, and cleaning up after they left. The women tried not to complain. If they did, they could be accused of destroying the Christmas Spirit.

With more men willing to clear away the leavings of the Christmas dinner and mop up after visitors, there is time for today's woman to participate in making an old-fashioned Christmas by marming around the place.

It was with the intention of having the best from the past and present that I found myself, with my family, in a home uninvited among twenty-five other people also uninvited. I had taken my cue from friends who had come to my place for Christmas dinner. They always spent what was left of Christmas Day visiting friends. "People expect this in Pasadena," they said.

The first couple we visited had sometimes shared Sunday dinner with us. It was getting close to five o'clock when we reached their home. We hesitated before ringing the doorbell. It was hard to knock ten years of Toronto acclimatization out of our systems. What if they had company, or were getting ready to go out the door with the same idea we had: to trot around from house to house? They were actually sitting to allow their later-than-midday Christmas dinner to settle. They would be on the go after we left. Maybe they would leave with us. Barry, who is a very humorous man, showed us the mug he got for Christmas – Number One Truck Driver. "That's next to nothing," he said. "Now, if I'd been number nine, I would have been next to Bo What's-Her-Name."

After chatting for a while, all of us left to visit elsewhere. Like a Pied Piper we kept adding on friends as we went from house to house. All through the night, each house we entered kept getting packed and repacked as people came and went.

We didn't need food after the Christmas dinner, but it did appear in every home. One lady took a frozen cake from the fridge, promising us it would melt in our mouths. I wanted to hang a sign around my neck: "Please don't feed me."

The best part of the night was kept until the end. One of my finest memories is of an old Salvationist couple singing with tears in their eyes as some of our group sang and played Christmas carols on the organ in the living room. Somewhere in the dimness of the old man's eyes I could see a memory taking shape – the memory of an old-fashioned Christmas.

Christmas Eve Night

Of the 365-366 days that fill a year, Christmas Eve shines the brightest and is chock full of expectancy. It begins the fifth season of the year: the people's season, one we get to decorate in spellbinding beauty. All across the world, there comes the slow withdrawal from the frenzy of gift buying. Lights go off in offices, mall parking lots become vacant as throngs disappear from the commercial scene. Hands join, hearts meet, and voices blend in the harmony of expectancy as people become part of something universal. From that first gift of Christmas, the Christ Child, came the people's custom of giving and receiving gifts on His birthday, creating a giant party.

Christmas Eve becomes the silent evening in the year – an event before the advent of the best day of the year. A light fall of snow is always ideal, hanging like a heavy silence in the heavens. It becomes an enclosing tranquility as it drops to the earth in a gentle drift of falling stars. Today, whenever I hear "Silent Night," I associate it with so many Christmas Eves in just that setting.

Instead of the traditional salted codfish and potatoes for Christmas Eve supper, I make apple sauce with bologna (not Bethle*ham*, as Sara, a little friend, called the Christmas ham); I grate potatoes and make latkes, explaining the menorah to the children. Christianity came out of Judaism, a huge part of my spiritual heritage. Side by side, Christianity and Hanukkah can join hands in a celebration of triumph.

Sometimes after supper we set up home movies, bringing back memories of when the children were small. We sip hot chocolates with marshmallows floating in them. Some of us try Michael's bonk drink: a concoction of Purity syrup, milk, and ice cream. Janalee tosses popcorn in the fireplace, just to hear it pop. I bring out the finest box of chocolates I was able to buy.

Christmas Eve holds a puncheon full of secrecy while our ears fill with sounds of song and music; prisms of colour dazzle our eyes; an ambrosia of treats draws our noses.

To the sounds of Christmas carols on the stereo, another sound is added. A long-distance call from a friend from "way back," and then another from a friend across the sea.

We go for a midnight walk, once the children are snug in their beds and flying through the night on wings of sleep.

A silent night descends amid snow falling, covering us in the ermine coat of this special night. Quietly we go, our feet pressing into the snow. Our laughter strikes the frosty air like Christmas bells. Each step takes us closer to Christmas Day.

We come home to lights twinkling on the fir tree beside a

fire dancing in the fireplace. Windows frame a world of softly falling snow polka-dotted in coloured lights. The taffeta rustle of paper goes *wrap* in the night as I finish a last-minute gift. I fill the stockings. The other half assembles a desk for Michael. Fathers don't need to make desks for their sons anymore. They can buy all the parts and the screws in one package and have a desk assembled in one hour if the instructions are not too difficult. Though it's easy to see a father hopping around like a rabbit trying to sniff missing screws lost in the carpet.

Finally, we put up our feet and lean back to listen to the crackle of the dying fire. On the mantel I've created the fantasy world of a ceramic village. A soft light glows from lamppost lanterns over angel hair snow. Figures of children, beautifully dressed in Christmas colours, hold hymnals as they stand beside white picket fences and trees.

By this time Christmas Day is already here, though daylight isn't. I turn off the winking tree lights and leave the black silhouette to guard the mysterious packages beneath it. Our cat, an out-of-this-world creature with only the green of its eyes showing, scampers away.

Outside, drops of rain pinhole perfect mounds of snow. Later, the best part will be nostalgia, as clear-cut as a diamond and as warm as a fire in the hearth.

Clausophobia

I had a deprived childhood brought on by, what Santa worshippers would describe as, depraved parents. They stuck to the religious aspects of Christmas like fingers to crazy glue, insisting that there was no room in Bethlehem for a chimerical fellow whose age was beginning to catch up with Methuselah, and his only line of communication was a simple-minded Ho, ho, ho!

My parents led me to believe that the few presents under the Christmas tree were from people I knew. If I did the math, I knew they were right. I could get a full night's sleep on Christmas Eve, instead of having to worry about Santa going missing in a snowstorm and taking my gifts with him. I didn't have to concern myself that a famous reindeer's snoot might fall off and Santa's entourage be thrown off course. I didn't have to fear that Santa might get stuck going down someone else's chimney, or have his butt burned to a crisp going down ours. I could be as naughty as I liked without a peeping Santa keeping record. I had already done my peeping, and I knew whatever gifts I would get were already tucked away in my parents' closet or packaged under the tree.

Having Santa Claus limited to a fairy tale had no adverse effect on my siblings and me. Children need to know that real people make Christmas happen, even while they share the fantasy of the season.

Today, parents can't tell their children there is no Santa Claus. He has been cloned all over the world – enough Santas to give us all Clausophobia. Once upon a time he was seen only in colouring books and on Christmas cards and wrapping paper, depicted in a long red robe, sometimes with a wreath on his head. Later, he was painted as a fat old man in a red suit smoking a black pipe to match his black belt and long, black rubbers. Now he has slimmed down and ditched the pipe. Moonlighting imposters of him have their pictures snapped with fans all over the world. Followers are happy to indulge their fantasies by writing to the "real" Santa at the North Pole by snail mail or email.

My children always saw Santa as a magical character: a symbol of the good in humans, just as I had known him as a child. Their eyes lit up when they saw him in stores, even while a little voice piped up, "Santa is a dressed-up man."

Once, when Michael was four, he was skipping through a shopping mall – his usual energetic self – when what did he see but Santa Claus in front of him, mouthing the authentic three-worder. Out went my credibility and in came his incredible ability to see this guy as the real Santa, or so I thought.

Later, I heard him tell a friend that he had seen Santa, and he was just a dressed-up man who couldn't name all the reindeer. He had tested him. His friend warned him that if he didn't believe in Santa he would get a lump of coal in his Christmas stocking. Michael told him that he had never seen coal so he'd like a lump. His sister scoffed at Santa having coal at the North Pole. She told Michael's young friend that Santa grew only chunks of ice there.

Believing in Santa as a fantasy didn't make him less real to Janalee. For children, reality and fantasy often merge. She, too, had imagined the patter of reindeer feet and a hearty Ho, ho, ho in the stillness of a Christmas Eve night.

Somewhere inside all of us there is the wish for a real live Santa Claus: someone who will give us something for nothing. What most of us really miss from Christmas is not faith in a generous old fellow from some hyperborean climate, but the loss of our childhood, and the fragility of its fantasies. We look for it in stores where simple little windup toys take us back to childhood pleasures. We buy gadget toys, hoping we will create memories for our children, not realizing, perhaps, that children create their own memories, real and imagined.

The Cabbage Patch Craze

The other day I saw a lone Cabbage Patch Kid sitting on a store shelf, and I thought: *How fickle the masses are*! I remember the year 1983, when the Christmas Spirit got a kick in the shins, groin, and wherever else it had a soft spot. Hordes of Christmas shoppers collided in stores all across the country, after being drawn together by an insane thread of green monster madness. It was the season when a pseudo–cabbage patch grew a crop of dimpled and dumpling faces and arms and legs.

The stampede over the dolls may have begun in one store as harried shoppers combed the shelves looking for the perfect gift. Perhaps the first ninety and eight customers gave the Cabbage Patch Kid only a glance. Who wanted a doll who had a blubbery-looking mug, cucumber arms, and pudding legs? The ninety-ninth person to see the doll may have gathered it to her breast and drooled over it, all the while exclaiming to the sales clerk that her little girl would be on cloud ninety-nine when she saw her very own kid. Likely, there was instant silence among the ninety-eight other customers. In fact, the Christmas music playing in the store may have instantly faded from shoppers' ears. One shopper, two shoppers, a flood of shoppers drew close as the kid was adopted, and wrapped. Soon there were only a few dolls left and more than a few people wanting them. They were bought while other customers swallowed hard. Suddenly everyone wanted something they couldn't have.

"There must be some kids left," protested one man, as his little girl sobbed against him. When the clerk murmured, "Sorry," she was grabbed and shaken so hard that her eyes rattled in their sockets. Even her throat got threatening looks as one incredibly muscled hulk ordered her to get more Cabbage Patch Kids – or else.

One man took a pen from his pocket and recorded the ruckus for a newspaper. Soon everybody was hearing about the Cabbage Patch Kids and how they grew – popular. Reporters with cameramen started looking into people's faces as they made their way to stores. If their eyes had a few flecks of green in them, along with a look of savage determination, the media followed the shoppers inside.

Suddenly parents everywhere wanted to become grandparents to Cabbage Patch Kids. They dragged their children into the stores and demanded that the clerks look the expectant young mothers straight in the eye and tell them there were no Cabbage Patch Kids left. In some stores where a few dolls had managed to survive the blitz, a rumour spread about their existence. Soon children were like china caught up in a bull ring stampede, trampled by a bunch of hysterical shoppers beating each other's features into the contortion of Cabbage Patch Kids' faces. One cameraman caught, first-hand, the agony, the whole agony, and nothing but the agony on the face of a little mother who'd had her kid ripped out of her arms by a nasty granny.

"Cabbage Patch Kidnapping!" yelled one woman.

A leg snapped on one young mother. She immediately said the rosary, thankful that it was her leg that had broken and not the leg of the Cabbage Patch Kid she was holding onto as if she were in the path of a cyclone.

In other stores, combatants crammed tight, turning their fists into weapons. Noses that once looked as pale as bakeapples were now the colour of Rudolph's nose as they came in contact with territorial fists. The Christmas Spirit got knocked out. Security was called in to revive him with a sprig of mistletoe and to help him back on his unsteady feet. At that moment, a woman who didn't have a child and never cared for dolls decided to give up the doll she had wanted only because someone else wanted it. Shoppers started to bid on it, even though it hadn't gotten to the checkout. One woman got the dibs on the doll by convincing the other bidders that her little dear had a terminal illness, and a Cabbage Patch Kid was the only thing that could cure her.

An old farmer, trying to get through the crowd to buy a shovel, yelled that the ugly critters should be thrown out with cabbage water. He got his tongue pulled on. "Ding dong, dog-gone," he muttered.

In one home, Mother and Father argued. "It's your fault," said Father, "that Tina wants that fat kid. All you women are turning into Barbie dolls with rigor mortis waiting to set in. Look at you – a Jane Fonda invention. Cheeks and bums are caving in all across the country. Next thing, Dolly Parton will be resizing her front. There's nothing comforting for a child to lean against anymore."

"Now, Tina," soothed Mother, "Baby Satina has all her dimples in the right places. Let's settle for her."

Little Tina would have none of it, and Father, after running out of tissues for her wet eyes, boarded a plane for London, where he had no trouble buying a Cabbage Patch Kid. He told lots of Londoners about the Canadian Cabbage Patch Kid frenzy, and how they could start their own Cabbage Patch Kid frenzy.

Craft shops were next hit by displays of hysterical fits. Jane Fonda would have been proud of the elbow bends, the facial twists, and the aerobic kicks displayed as mothers became tailors overnight, producing their own Cabbage Patch Kids in nine days, or nine hours, depending on the amount of energy being worked off as their sewing machines hummed: "I am dreaming of a Cabbage Patch Kid Christmas." Soon, shoppers geared up to fight over the question of which Cabbage Kids were real and which ones were impersonators.

The Cabbage Patch Kid craze made headlines in newspapers across the world: Of the 500,000 children who held out arms to adopt a Cabbage Kid, only 300,000 were successful. The other 200,000 remained Kidless.

This year, the Cabbage Patch Kid can be seen sitting on store shelves here and there, like wallflowers. Sometimes a young mother whose mother risked losing an eyeball to get her a dimpled, dumpling Cabbage Patch Kid might pick up a doll, as a spurt of nostalgia kicks in. She remembers when her mother and other shoppers were squeezed within an inch of their lives as they tried to cling to a Cabbage Patch Kid in the all-out Cabbage Patch wars.

The Christmas Caller

The call came on a Saturday morning, a week before Christmas. The voice on the line sounded like that of an older man. "I've dialled the wrong number," he explained.

I agreed. Then on impulse, I said, "Merry Christmas."

I was stopped from hanging up when he answered, "Merry Christmas, me darlin', but it's not really merry." He rushed on. "No one wants you to drop in anymore, and if you come you must knock first. And when you do go anyplace, there's all these instructions: Take off your boots, wipe your feet, do this, don't do that."

I understood his gripe. Don't we all! We are all a part of it. Finally I said goodbye to the old fellow.

I was sitting in my office just after supper, and the warm glow of the lamp made me feel encompassed by the warmth of Christmas as the strains of "Silent Night," from the next room, drifted into my ears.

Tintinnabulation! It was "him" again on the phone. Warning bells went off. I've had a few calls that have turned my grey matters into red bleeps in the past. But it was Christmas. I'd take the risk.

"I've got the wrong number," he said without a show of regret.

I suggested he ask the operator to put him through to the number he wanted. He agreed on this; then he kept on talking. I'd already been taken away from my writing too many times already, and I had about an hour before I'd leave to visit friends. But I didn't want him to think I was in a rush. I gave him some time to talk. I finally had to go. Telephone operators can tell you that a lot of older people call them this time of the year, just to talk.

My Christmas caller made me think of my mother and her frequent mid-morning long-distance calls just to see how I was. It was really her effort to make contact and dispel the feelings of loneliness in a house that had lost its children.

I didn't know what I was letting myself in for, chatting with a stranger. But when the man called again Sunday afternoon I let him talk. The flu bug had bitten me and I'd just crawled into bed, my head feeling as heavy and as dense as a brick. My throat felt like sandpaper. It was an effort for me to talk. I did a few sidesteps around the man's personal questions, and let him go on about his own life. I learned that his wife was dead and he lived alone. He told me about the time he spent in Windsor – about the little girl he helped raise. I couldn't believe my ears. He was talking about a cousin of mine. I met her for the first time when I was seventeen and spending a year in Windsor.

"Her mother was some skate," he said, "floozing around, leaving her children to grow up on their own."

Her father was my uncle. He died in his thirties, probably due to a shock he received one fall morning when he went bird hunting. Night was just scattering when he went over the hills. Two brothers happened to be on the hills at the time. They could imitate a partridge – which they did when they saw my uncle coming. They lifted their white mittens (the colour of the partridge in the fall) and moved over the barrens. My uncle shot at them. The fright from what he'd done affected his health, along with the strain of bringing one of the men home on his shoulders. The men weren't seriously injured, but my uncle died about four months later.

According to my caller, my cousin lived with a family in Bishop's Falls. She was treated harshly, and one day while she was in Windsor, he met her. He asked her if she was hungry, and she told him she was starving. When he asked her what she'd like, she had answered shyly, "A tin of beans." He said he gave her the money to buy it. According to him, he and his wife took the eleven-year-old and raised her. If his story is true, my cousin has a lot of Christmases to thank him for.

"I'm sorry for getting the wrong number – again," he said, and hung up.

Actually, he didn't get the wrong number. All he had wanted was someone's voice and ear.

My Christmas caller is one in thousands of lonely people in the world. Sure, he could become a pest. That's how some of us see lonely people who are reaching out during this fast-moving season to rid themselves of that long-distance feeling.

I should bake my Christmas caller some Christmas sweet-bread.

O Christmas Tree

When my two children were still in the roost, the first tree in our living room was crafted, and displayed on the wall. It held twenty-five pockets, and, from the first day of December, it provided the incentive to spread out Halloween candy until Christmas. The children counted off the days by the number of pockets still bulging. I hoped they wouldn't be tempted into thinking they could shorten the countdown to Christmas Day by flattening a few pockets prematurely.

I always restrained myself from getting into the Christmas spirit too soon. But by November, with the American Thanksgiving holiday out of the way, and Santa Claus parades in full swing, it was hard not to be awakened to the advent of another Christmas.

I got the scent of Christmas early one year. Heads turned when I murmured that we should look for a Christmas tree.

"In September!" the two children exclaimed in unison. The consensus was that Mom had flipped her hood.

One year, Christmas sounds came earlier than September.

In mid-August, I was stopped in my tracks by the strains of "I'm Dreaming of a White Christmas" coming over the airwaves. My first reaction was: "I'm dreaming!" To wake myself I turned up the radio volume and flung open the door. "Do you hear what I hear?" I called to the kids outside. They nodded, wide-eyed. And there, clad in shorts and halter tops, the sun hot and bothering, they demanded that the Christmas tree be hoisted immediately.

It is usually October by the time I attempt to gather the clan for an all-out tree search. I try to find the perfect tree and tie a ribbon, bells – or whatever – on it, so that when we go staggering through snow-laden woods, our snow-wrapped tree will be waving a come-hither sign, or, with the help of a little wind, ring-a-linging its bells. Besides, it's hard to pick and choose a tree when we are knee-deep in snow, and falling headfirst more often than not. The Christmas weatherman has a track record for being mean just when we've been on a tree-finding mission. If the day is mild and bright, there can be other surprises. On one trek, I stepped on pure white snow and my leg went down through it into a muddy hole. I felt an icy grasp on my foot. As I pulled my leg free, muck splattered over my white sock and the pristine snow. Before I bent to retrieve the boot left behind, I looked around; I didn't want to come up under the belly of a moose. I'm not paranoid. There are people in these parts who tell stories of having been draped on moose antlers, or goosed by them. Others have come close to being hugged by black bears.

We usually bring home a tree that is too big for our living room. We have to cut, shape – and conceal its amputated look. White ends like broken bones. The woodsman of the house is adept at chopping off the top and leaving it like a *V*, needing to be squeezed until it's a number one. One year I lifted my dainty angel and slipped it down over the long, spiky, inverted *V*. The angel looked down on me from her lofty perch as if to ask, "How would you like to be impaled on the top of a tree?" As soon as I let go of the branch, she flew off the tree and landed on the carpet, where she lay face down, her halo twisted, a wing broken. I don't talk to angels, but this one clearly needed a pick-me-up pep talk.

The angel was soon mended and the tree decorated. A woodsy scent permeated the room as icicles danced and sparkled against the glow of coloured lights. At that moment, Christmas became a scent, a faint drift of essence flooding the room. Michael soon had the Nativity scene renovated. He laid carpet on the stable floor and built an extension – a garage for Joseph's car, a present from this century. Icicles were soon hanging off Michael's hair and the cat's fur. Everywhere the cat went an icicle was sure to follow. At one point she had an ornament swinging from her tail. It put the cat in action like a windup toy. Icicles followed my heels like tails or settled into the carpet until they got sniffed up by the vacuum cleaner.

The other half made a point that we didn't have to go running around in the wild looking for a tree among half-cocked moose hunters. An artificial tree would do, and it would keep its needles. "It may not keep its branches," I told him. "When the cat decides to sleep on them, they often break off." I was referring to the dainty artificial tree we'd set up one year. It was pretty from a distance, but it lacked scents. One branch lost a screw and I pushed a lollipop stick through the hole between the branch and the tree. It held until the cat tried to sit on the branch, and she got dropped on her hiney.

One year, I gritted my teeth, determined not to give in to the impulse to go hunt down a real, live tree. The children were at the stage in their lives when they would not have minded seeing a fully-trimmed tree dragged out of a walk-in closet. I may have been talked into letting an artificial tree give me my Christmas glow if I had not been sitting by the fireplace one night reading from my Christmas manuscript, *The Gift of Christmas*. Sentimental juice coursed through my veins, and I was inspired. I find it hard not to be contemplative when I meander down memory lane to the barren outport where I grew up. I caught the scent of fir only after my father went away from the cove on Christmas Eve and brought back a freshly cut tree. He dragged it, snow and all, into the front room, filling the place with a tangy, fresh aroma, different from the wafts of salty air I was used to. The tree scent permeated the red and green tissue paper wrapping the gifts under the tree.

That memory got me on the hunt again for a new Christmas tree. I reminded myself of the time we went into the woods, and the wind showed itself in sheets of snow and ran nasty cold needles up and down our spines. I had run and hidden in the car, which looked and felt like an igloo. This time we visited a grocery store to buy one of the trees propped against the outside wall. The other half tried to haul a tree from where it was leaning against the building. It was stuck in ice. He pulled and twisted it, branches flopping and banging against him as if he and the tree were having a fight. He stood it up and I could see right through the sparse branches. Another tree looked like a reindeer up on its hind legs.

"Where will we put the decorations, or will we need any?" I asked, a little disillusioned. I had an image of a tree beside the fireplace, its branches thick enough to hold a cat in bed for the night. I pulled on a fat tree. This one cost more, but it had something to work with. It could be trimmed and shaped.

"Okay, then," the other half offered. "The fat one is too big to get into the house, but we can trim the fat." He eyed the top. "It will have to be cut off."

"Not from the top," I said, moving to check out another tree. "This tree is perfect!" I exclaimed. "Its branches don't wave or flop, and it won't tickle you in the armpits or reach around your back for a hug when you lean in to put on the angel treetop." One year I had to hang heavy trinkets so that the branches would drop enough to conceal a gap, after we had twirled the tree like a ballerina to give us its best side.

This tree was like a hostage refusing to get into the trunk of the car. We grabbed it, pushed it, threatened to leave it out in the cold, but it wouldn't budge. We finally crumped it in, shedding a few of its needles. It bobbed against the line tying it down as we took it home. My fingers were frozen and I thought of the eighteen-year-old whose snowmobile had broken down a few hundred yards from homes in the vicinity. He had broken down at a time when the power had gone off. He assumed he wasn't near any homes, and he went the wrong way. I could feel his chill, and felt sorry he hadn't made it home to the lights of Christmas.

The tree was left standing on its head by the house for two days to let it dry off and to make it fuller. Dog tracks led me to sniff for doggy-tree habits. When I went to bring the tree inside, ice still decorated it like icing on a cake. What to do? I plugged in a hair dryer and blew its branches dry. Some ice let go, but some was still carried into the house. It left puddles in the plastic I had laid below it. The cat lapped up the water.

A wrapped beef bucket holding pebbles and water could not coax the tree into keeping its needles. They fell, not one by one, nor two by two. The slightest touch, and needles sprayed the floor like hailstones. They had obviously been frozen on. Stray needles stood straight up in the carpet, waiting for our unsuspecting soles. The tree began turning yellow-green like an old bruise. Before Old Christmas Day, we started undressing it of its decorations and lights.

We learned it was best to cut our own tree and, after our children were grown, we had more fun by adding the grand-kidlings to the outing.

"We're going to mark our Christmas trees," I told Nicholas, the oldest grandkidling.

"It's good I brought a black marker," he said, pulling one from his pocket.

Off we went through the woods on a warm autumn day. I trudged behind the other half, a grown kidling and two grand-kidlings. Clarence, Janalee, and Nicholas were ahead. Soon Joshua was tailing me.

We lit a fire and made tea. As smoke danced above our campfire, blackjacks came for a Thanksgiving dinner of pieces of cobble bread and chocolate chip pancakes.

Janalee picked her tree very carefully. (She did not want to take the life of more than one tree.) We soon had two trees marked, one with Nicholas's black marker. The other, close to it, was scarfed by discarded pantyhose.

December came and we went to get our trees: one for each house. Snow swirled around us as we drove in over a bumpy and snow-covered woods road. We parked, and soon branches came alive as we shook away snow. The children fell into fat white soft-ness, and lifted themselves out of it, confettied in white.

"The snow is too deep, Nanna. Everyone is making too big steps," Joshua complained as he grabbed at twigs to pull himself out of the holes he had gotten himself into. Like me, he fell flat on his face a few times.

"Are you still alive?" Joshua asked the black-marked tree, giving it a shake. Nicholas scorned his question. "Trees aren't alive. They don't move by themselves or anything."

"They grow up," Joshua said, "unless people cut them down."

Now was the time for a forestry lesson. The cartographer in the family was chosen to give the grandkidlings the low-down on trees while they did a hearty roll in the snow. Snow angels would not have recognized themselves. Soon, hot breaths swirled and mingled with the steam from hot chocolate as we eyed our trees tied to the rack on the car.

With the trees up and decorated, and Heintje singing "O Christmas tree," I sat remembering all our Christmas tree outings. They and the trees we marked – especially the one with the black marker – were as perfect as could be.

Father Christmas Unmasked

Gertie grew up in the 1920s in Island Cove, a small outport with a beach lapped by the sea. On a high-rise strip of land was a spread of saltbox houses flanked by woods holding thick fir trees. No one thought to bring the trees indoors and decorate them. There were no coloured lights. Only the soft glow of lamplight filled windows in cozy homes, their fires fuelled by firewood. The cove people had seen a sketch of Father Christmas only on Christmas cards, and not often.

The small isolated community, reached only by boat or horse and sleigh, had no Christmas catalogues. But word had gotten out that there was a Father Christmas and that he brought gifts to children on Christmas Day.

"'Twasn't like it is now," says Gertie, "with Santa Claus in every mall. The only *maul* we knowed anything about was the kind used to drive a stake in the ground.

"Sure, there's no Christmas like an old Christmas. We had fun down in Island Cove. We had Christmas for twelve days. Now kids got it from September to January, but it's all harassment, everyone wondering what to buy everyone else, and how to better the other person with the best present. When I was a girl, a schooner showed up in the spring of the year to take Father and the rest of the men in the cove to Labrador. They went by sail with the wind taking them where it wanted to, with only glasses to go by. They were gone from June to September, and when they finished fishing in the fall of the year, they came home with the fish salted down. They spent all fall washing and drying the fish on flakes. Besides that, we had a horse, a cow, sheep, and pigs, and we grew our living on the point. When the fish was cured, the men packed it back in the schooner and took it to St. John's. The skipper took half of the voyage, and the merchant took half of what was left for the fishermen.

"The men sailed back home, then they and their women left for Northern Bight Station (Goobies) to catch the train to St. John's for winter supplies. They brought back ever so many pounds of rolled oats for three cents a pound. They unloaded wooden boxes of tea, and butter, barrels of flour, kegs of molasses. We'd have raisins, and sweets in wrappers to be kept for Christmas. The men brought back four- and five-gallon kegs, with molasses sugar on the bottom, as cheap as dirt. They used the molasses sugar and yeast to run off moonshine for the Twelve Days of Christmas. The moonshine was made after midnight when no unwanted visitor was likely to show. We had a back door that led to the woods, should the moonshiner need to make a quick run.

"Preparations were made around the house inside and out. Cakes were baked heavy and succulent with raisins, spices, mixed fruit, rum, and molasses. The scent of Christmas baking went all through the house, rising up the stairs to bedrooms where the children lay dreaming of getting something in their stocking."

By Christmas Eve, Gertie and her brothers and sisters were all excited about Christmas Day. The Christmas dinner: a male goat or a pig was slaughtered. Sometimes a goose or a turkey was killed and plucked. Kindling was stowed in porch lockers, the hunting guns were placed in their racks, and the homemade wine, birch beer, and moonshine were ready. Hooked and braided mats were washed and dried, and floors were scrubbed. Then, after the family had finished a scoff of molasses bread, and boiled salted salmon, their mother cleaned the stove and iron kettle with black polish. She stirred her kettle of berry hocky and strained it into cups, sweetening it for a delicious drink. Vamps were hung on the bedposts for the children. What was in each vamp sometimes served as the only Christmas gift.

Christmas Eve was only the beginning of a twelve-day season to look forward to. With the wood laid in and the moonshine out, the men went on the idle while women still served, and mopped pools of water and mud behind company who spent the night in booted dances, cracking jokes, telling ghost stories and riddles while helping themselves to a taste of the missus's hospitality and the mister's grog. Children watched adults become children again, and dressed up for the best bit of fun they had all year, laced with a bit of Christmas cheer.

One Christmas Eve, Gertie and her siblings got a big surprise when a knock came on the door. No one in the cove ever knocked on anyone else's door before walking in. The only knocks anyone had ever noted were a succession of three raps. Such an event foretold the death of a person in the community. This time there was only one knock, and then the children all looked up as a strange figure filled the porch. In the soft lamplight that shadowed the porch, a figure standing in front of the children was an imposing sight. The creature was dressed in a red robe, and wearing a white cloth over his face and a black cap.

Gertie wasn't old enough to know that the real Father Christmas always showed his face. This figure came like the first Christmas mummer of the Twelve Days of Christmas, but he didn't speak like one.

"Ho, ho, ho!" he called. The children looked shocked at the sight of Old St. Nick so close. Except for Gertie, who was sitting on the inside of the table with Uncle Ike (who lived with the family), all the children scampered upstairs to get away from the masked man whose *Ho, ho, ho!* followed them. Gertie squinched when Father Christmas came into the kitchen, close enough to hold out a handful of candy. She was scared, thinking that maybe it was one of her neighbours dressed up. He had killed a pig, and when she saw him scraping it, he threatened to take out the pork chops and sew her up inside the pigskin.

She cautiously reached her hand; then she pulled it back.

"Go ahead," Uncle Ike urged her. Then he looked at the man and said, "Knock off your foolishness with that child," as if he was acquainted with the stranger. Gertie thought him brazen to speak in this manner to Old St. Nick. For sure, he would never darken their door again after such an unwelcome! Father Christmas ignored Uncle Ike and held out his hand again. This time Gertie cautiously lifted a candy from his hand. Then he thumped his way upstairs. Gertie grinned, imagining the children leaping on their feather beds and moving against the wall, afraid of him.

Father Christmas, coming as the first Christmas mummer on Christmas Eve, became a tradition. If the children were upstairs when his black-mittened fist hit the door, they would all come running back down for candy. From under his red outfit, the old fellow pulled candy from a bag and filled each little hand. Norman, Gertie's younger brother, wanted more. He held out both hands. Father Christmas filled only one. Then he left.

Cyril, Gertie's older brother, was bolder than the other children. He scoffed at the idea of Santa coming in a sleigh hauled through the skies by reindeer. He wasn't sure he believed in reindeer either. He had never seen one. One Christmas, he decided that it was about time Old St. Nick showed his face. He was sure he was nothing more than a common mummer from the cove. He hit upon a bold plan. One Christmas, the children sat on the bed waiting for the old gent's step on the stairs. When he came into the bedroom, the girls squealed.

Old St. Nick reached out his hand with candy, and when the candy was safely in Cyril's hand, he reached his other hand to grab the false face. From Father Christmas's gait, and by the look of his boots, Cyril had gotten suspicious. He had unmasked Arthur Will, the children's father.

"I knowed 'twas he," Cyril called in triumph.

"Could be his twin," Beatrice, his youngest sister, said, not willing to give up Old St. Nick.

Father Christmas beat a hasty retreat down the stairs.

"Now we've lost our treats," Annie wailed.

"We'll find them in our stockings," Cyril promised.

The next morning, there were sweets in each stocking. Gertie remembers a red ribbon in hers, used to tie a red bow in her hair.

Father Christmas didn't show his face, masked or otherwise, in the cove ever again, but the mummers did. They came knocking loudly and screeching, "Any mummers allowed in?" When they got in, they ordered a tip of moonshine, which was given only after they threw up their false faces.

Gertie, now eighty-eight, is well and spry. Just as night is scattering on Christmas Eve morning, she is in her kitchen cutting up salmon, and codfish, and peeling potatoes for the thirteen family members coming for supper. When she finishes her work, she sits for a spell. She leans back in her chair, folds her arms and says, "I always said that Cyril took Santa Claus. We missed him, we did. But we still got the candy. The only thing that changed was that Father stayed in the house all Christmas Eve.

"Now Father is gone. Annie, Cyril, and Norm are all gone. Santa Claus – he's around yet. Still, there's no Christmas like an old Christmas."

It's The Thought That Counts

All of us have received a gift with this tag-on comment from the giver: "It isn't much – but it's the thought that counts."

Sometimes the thought doesn't count for much, especially when a gift is given for the sake of giving a gift, rather than for the purpose of giving the receiver pleasure.

When I was in school, I remember one time when the teacher had us pick the name of another child from a basket holding the names of all the children. Each child was responsible for bringing a present to school for the pupil whose name she picked. These presents were often exchanged anonymously.

When my brother's name was called, Johnny grinned and strolled up to take his present from the teacher's extended hand. His face was already settling into disappointment as he walked back to his seat. There was a familiar feel to the shape inside brown wrapping paper held with white shop string. Everyone else's present was wrapped in red or green tissue paper and tied with green or red twine. Johnny ran his tongue around his dry lips as he, urged on by the other children, pulled off the string. Out fell a pencil and a scribbler – school supplies he laid eyes on every day of the school week. He could count on his mother buying these items when it wasn't Christmas. For a moment he looked as if he would cry. Instead, he eyed the other pupils hugging their gifts to their chests. Then he got up and left the school, even though the pupils had not been dismissed for the day.

I followed, knowing that Johnny would like to tear the scribbler to pieces and crack his pencil on the nose of whoever gave him this common present.

"Here," I offered, "you can have mine."

He looked down at my car-shaped pencil sharpener and shook his head no.

"It's the thought that counts," my mother said.

I realized then that there is very little thought put into some gifts, and very little care given to the presentation. If it was the thought that counted, it was counted in five cents for the scribbler and one cent for the pencil. The thought would count if the present was something Johnny valued, and if the child who gave it could not have done better.

Some "thought that counts" gifts turn out to be good for a laugh. When I first met the man who would become my husband, he knew nothing about me. On Christmas Eve, he and his cousin came bearing gifts to my cousin's and my apartment. He gave me a box of maraschino cherry chocolates (cherries I hate), while my roommate's date brought her chocolate-coated almonds (almonds I love). The exchange was mutual. Ruby took my cherries and I took her nuts, unlike the first time she and I met the two cousins: my date had been more to her taste and she had tried to switch him and her date.

Unfortunately for her, trading chocolates was more to my taste. The gift that counted came on the next Christmas Eve, in something smaller than a chocolates box. Inside was an engagement ring that was slipped on my finger as I sat beside the Christmas tree in a second-hand designer dress – blue satin with rhinestones on the belt and puffed sleeves – bought at the now famous Honest Ed's store.

Before Christmas last year, at a wedding shower, I won a prize. No one noticed the impish smile on my face as I opened the wrappings to find a box of cherry chocolates. When I got home, I rewrapped them and put them under the tree for the other half.

"What's this?" he asked, puzzled.

"Maybe they are the cherry chocolates you gave me on our first Christmas Eve."

"I thought you'd forgotten about that."

"You thought – and it is the thought that counts," I teased, adding, "you're the chocolate coating the nut."

Gran Kennedy was once given a white, blue-brimmed demitasse cup and saucer. On the cup, in gold letters, were the words "Love the Giver." Those times when we are the recipients of a Christmas gift that is not to our fancy, we can love the giver – despite the gift. Sometimes it really is the thought that counts.

You Can Go Home Again

One year, when the children were small, I sighed, "Too bad we couldn't get home for Christmas."

The oldest offspring looked at me and asked, "What do you call this place?"

I tried to explain that it's home away from home. The house my father built is the place where I was conceived, born, and raised. It is still home. I can't expect children who have lived in many different places in their short lifetime to understand that it takes many years of being lived-in for a house to get beyond an embryonic stage and gain a soul.

In spite of the expression "You can't go home again," many of us, without hitching our hides to Santa's reindeer, go home every Christmas. We go home to the past from an arm-chair by pressing the mind's nostalgic button. Memory allows us to travel through time and space. Like wine, the more aged the Christmas past is, the more we enjoy it.

I go home, if only in my heart, home to cliffs and sea and family. It's Christmas Eve and my older siblings and I go past our home – a bungalow nestled in the hills beside the pond – down a gravelled, roller-coaster road to our father's boyhood home by the sea in Hibb's Cove. Brittle snow crunches under our feet on the way to Gran Kennedy's house. It is a night when the whole world seems to sing of mystery and majesty. Snowflakes fall like millions of particles of peace, bedding like a soft gentleness inside our beings.

John, Betty, and I hurry up Esau Porter's Hill, and cross Cliff Path, where a lone shaft of light beams out a pathway across the sea, a living thing that, when it isn't groaning and roaring, is slapping gently against the stageheads, and sucking on their old, grey wooden legs. I stand under the glow of Cliff Path's light. The thrashing and mournful breaking of the sea brings loneliness. It is as if we've entered its world, its cold as keen as its mystery; the air comes against my skin as if the ocean is breathing in my face, the wind off it touching my lips with soft, cold fingers; its whispers breathe against my ears, as if from an ancestor who has stepped from the grave to bring voices of those who have lived and gone in centuries past. I feel caught in an eternity; its timelessness fills me; its immortality holds me.

In from 100-foot cliffs, under the drop of Kennedy Hill, in a peaked two-storey house, Gran Kennedy is expecting us. Pappa Kennedy died before I was born. John opens a gate and, with snow and pebbles crunching under our feet, we walk up the steep lane and turn the corner to Gran's house. As we kick our snow-caked boots against the steps of the bridge, we see Gran through the window. She is sitting on a brown settle beneath a wall of Christmas cards. They hang like loose, uneven bricks. She always receives a lot of cards, some with stuffed satin bells, glittering trees, or ribboned fronts. She doesn't think that the five cents postage is too much to pay to keep a line of communication open between friends and relatives.

As Betty lifts the latch to go in, Gran turns her head to the sound. A smile crosses her lips and follows the soft curves of her cheeks. She rubs her hand down her bibbed apron and rises from her position like a latter-day Victorian queen, ramrod straight, and hurries toward the door. Betty opens it, and the warmth from the kitchen stove touches our cold faces. Gran's cheeks lift round and full as she greets us with a wide smile. We wish her a Merry Christmas and put our presents into her hands.

She offers us Christmas cake and a choice of clingy that comes from a Purity syrup bottle, or swanky, made from juicy cranberries picked from the hills the spring before, after a winter's frost gave them their sweetness. When we tell her we'd like some swanky, she goes to the cupboard under a row of old-fashioned jugs and brings out a bottle of cranberry jam, specially preserved for this festive drink. She heaps the bottom of the glass with the jam and then she pours in hot water. Like magic, a strong, rosy hue fills the glass. The warmth of the drink produces a lighthearted feeling in me that is as intoxicating as the excitement of Christmas. Its scent reminds me of the times I picked black, blue, and red berries on the hills of the cove when the grass was green and the sea was gentler and the air was filled with warm sunlight.

Gran gives us our Christmas boxes and we hurry out the door, down the lane, and up Cliff Path, snow springing up like scattering diamonds around our feet. I stop on Cliff Path and stand still, caught in a snow globe. Voices call, "Come on," cracking the globe. My feet and time move on, and the sounds of the sea become distant.

Multi-striped hard-knobbed candy fill our mouths – Gran's parting gift from her big apron pocket. We quicken our steps toward home, hoping the Christmas lights will be on the tree in the bay window and poking through the night like polka dots.

Dad goes away early every Christmas Eve afternoon to cut the tree. He returns with it, dragging it into the house. Then he shapes it the way he wants it – sawing and drilling holes in the trunk and inserting branches to give the tree perfect symmetry.

Then, before the tree can be decorated, he spends hours getting the two sets of lights in working order. This always takes a miracle, considering that some of the sockets are cracked and corroded, wires frayed and their connections broken. The younger children wait, breath held in as Dad tries the lights. Believing that Christmas is a season of faith, they never doubt that soon the room will be lit in a spectrum of candlelight. The bubbling, water-filled electric candles always give warmth to the cold room, making it as cozy as a kitchen with a boiling kettle on the stove.

We hurry up the road toward the house and the sight of the Christmas tree standing in the window, highlighting water drops on the windowpanes as if they are lustrous pearls. We go inside and lay the mysterious presents under the tree.

There is a box of ornaments, but not enough to go around and up and down the tree. We fold sheets of coloured paper, or pages from the Christmas catalogues. We cut down through folded paper not quite to the end; then we open the sheets lengthwise and glue them together to make globes for the tree. Dolls from white or red yarn, or fans from coloured paper, complete the decorated tree. It is my job to place the paper créche at the base. Mary and Joseph are getting a little worse for wear, but the fiery red bulb, hung above the manger, creates a magical aura. The time will come when I will place my own créche, with its heavy carved figures, under the tree. It is because I enjoy the paper one so much that mine will have such significance, ensuring the continuity of a memory.

My siblings' and my excitement is bridled by our mother's calm manner as she shoos us off to bed. The younger children are already asleep. My sister and I lie in the darkness and indulge our imagination, listening to parental whispers blending with the sound of soft rustling green and red tissue wrapping paper. In the fever of expectancy, we finally succumb to sleep.

The Christmas fairy creeps into our room and lays a

ribbed brown stocking at the foot of the bed. They are stockings Betty and I wear winter and summer. In winter, the stockings are always pulled high and held with garters, while in the heat of a summer day they are, sometimes, rolled down like doughnuts around our white legs. Now the stockings are bulging with goodies. Sometimes we stir from sleep in time to see our mother steal away.

Christmas always comes slipping in through the night like an angel of promise touching our jittery lids, lifting us wide awake to ignore the semi-darkness as the pungent scent of oranges wrapped in soft tissue paper and the sweet ambrosia of pointed apples drifts to our noses. My sister and I jump to the cold canvas floor and dance from foot to foot in rhapsodical unison, the cold shooting excitement deeper into our bones. We quickly empty our stockings, exclaiming over some unexpected trinket stuffed among the fruit and candy. Next, we hurry to the tree and open our gifts while our tired, Christmas-rushed parents, still in bed, listen to our childish exclamations and smile, remembering some Christmases from their past.

Dad remembers the 1920s, when he and his siblings hung their stocking on Christmas Eve, New Year's Eve, and Old Christmas Day. "The stock was dwindling on the last of it and we got only a piece of Christmas cake: moist and drenched in rum from the rum barrels our father kept." He remembers getting lead soldiers from Blanche Lear, his godmother, on Christmas morning. Another Christmastime, he found a pair of red rubber boots hanging on the glass doorknob downstairs. Mom remembers getting a rag doll. Another time she got an angora tam, and a child's enamel tea set that had cost her father ninety-eight cents. In the 1930s, a rocking horse cost $2.98, and a Lionel electric train could be had for $8.98. These prices were still out of the reach of families who made little money.

My grandparents, Elizabeth and Jacob, didn't exchange gifts. The only things they ever got in their stockings were what they put in them – their feet. There were stories of an occasional mouse . . .

By mid-morning, we are stuffed like little turkeys, and the enjoyment of the big turkey and its trimmings is left to the eager adults. We are more interested in making surreptitious visits to the tree in the front room. The door is opened only to let us go in by the Christmas tree for a look, and to draw in the scent of fir permeating the cold air. The huge box of assorted chocolates under the tree draws me like a magnet, and I often sneak a sweet nougat. The temptation is short-lived. I'm not the only child who has those irresistible urges, for the box is soon emptied, much to my mother's dismay.

There comes a time when children spill out of the family home and scatter to build other homes and families, to come back together with brothers and sisters and parents for scoffs and guffaws. Joking, participating in brainteasers, and carrying on theological debates with brothers brings a stimulating end to the old year. The laughter that comes with family gatherings is as buoying as bottled spirits and leaves only pleasant hangovers.

I go home again to a father and mother who are not so quick on their feet. That strong fisherman, who designed and built boats with a precision that almost took a fisheries inspector's breath away, is gone. In his place has come a stooped old man with faltering gait, as if he is coming from the woods, carrying on his back, as in times past, a bent log that will be scarfed into the keel of a new boat.

Now, under the mantel he plugs in the little tree that he made from coat hangers. Mom has been left with crippling arthritis. She can no longer lift the turkey from the oven, but she can stir the gravy into a succulent treat. I know they will both soon leave the house by Pond Road.

Then that time comes. Mom sits in her rocking chair, waiting for me. I have promised to come for her last Christmas at home. I open the door, and plant a kiss on her soft cheek. Dad is no longer on the daybed reading his Bible, the *Reader's Digest*, or *The Compass*. He lost the use of his legs a week before Christmas, was placed in the hospital, and from there to a senior citizens' nursing home.

Finally, my parents are in their new home away from home, on their way to their eternal home. Dad is drifting, waking. Mom is adjusting, remembering – going home in her mind . . .

The house is empty, as empty as it was so many years ago when I came home from school to find that Mom had gone "making" fish and helping in some other family chore outside the home. From the stage I often watched for the sign of the boat coming home from the cape. At first it was a tiny smudge as small as a loo on water, and then it grew larger, as if the seascape were painting its own scene of Dad, his brothers Jim and Golden, their oldest offspring, and the skiff riding the waves. The smudge became detailed, and finally the fishermen's glad faces came into view. Soon they would open pounds full of fish to the delight of the family.

My grandparents' house in the cove is gone. The lane up to Gran's and Pappa's house and the footprints they (Elizabeth and Jacob) and their family made in the earth are gone. The path down to the stagehead, where fish were landed for several generations, has been obliterated. Beyond my grandparents' time and place, the world has changed more than they could have imagined.

I leave Port de Grave, go past "the harbour," where Christmas lights are strung from boat to boat in a dazzling myriad, lit each December by those who go down to the sea in ships to face the strength of wind and sea. In song and music, fishermen bow before the humble manger scene to remember the great fisher of men and to accept the gift of Christmas.

I go home to Pasadena, my home, sweet home in the beautiful, snow-decorated Humber Valley. I hang Christmas stockings on the hooks my father placed there when he built the mantel for my fireplace. I watch flickering flames light up the faces of a family I helped create, and I am contented. But now and then I wish I could go down to the sea again, to the lonely cove that is sometimes wild, and all I want is the sound of the sea, a Cliff Path light, and the taste of Gran Kennedy's swanky and sweets, to bring me home to childhood Christmases.

Instead, I turn on the television and the family pins their eyes to Charles Dickens's *A Christmas Carol*. If that isn't enough, we watch *It's a Wonderful Life* and think about how each person becomes a character in the story of the people who begot us, and how different life would be for others if we weren't here.

The gift of nostalgia remains a priceless gift that is never used up with remembering, never worn enough to discard. It remains as sweet as the clingy and swanky Gran served, and the mulled cranberry drink from Second Cup my mother and I have enjoyed, and as rich as the iced cappuccinos we have often brought our parents from Tim Hortons.

From a Bethlehem stable to today's secular and spiritual celebrations, we stir up forgotten times with family, friends, and old acquaintances.

The trinity of faith, hope, and charity brings a powerful surge of well-being as we unwrap the gift of Christmas over and over.

The ambulance was waiting and my father bravely donned the Irish cap I had bought him from a booth beside Cahir Castle,

Ireland. He would never get to Ireland, though in his mind he had seen the green, green grass of Ireland, the home of Irish ancestors who had gone home again only in their minds. My father was leaving the house he built fifty-five years ago, leaving the outport he was born in almost eighty-three years before. His wide, sad eyes were his words. He knew he would not be coming home, and he would not light the little Christmas tree he had constructed after he could no longer handle a large tree. Beside him on the night table in the nursing home was a holly tree I had brought him, its red berries reminding him of the ripe berries he had often picked from the hills. His mind would hold the memories of the cove, carry them until the light of his life went out, as it did on January 21, my son's birthday. Now he lies in motherland, overlooking the sea through which he travelled home in storms and in calms. I now carry his memories inside mine. I can go home with them.

Christmas Is A Birthday

Celebrating Jesus's birthday is our way of telling God we accept Divine Love gift-wrapped in a human being.

Taking Christ Out Of Christmas

When Michael was five, he looked up at me one day and asked, "Mommy, was Jesus born on His birthday?"

Instead of responding with a flippant answer that no one is born on his birthday (we are all a year old by the time we have our first birthday), I told him that we don't know when Jesus was born. He *was* born and that's what's important for all the people around the world who celebrate His birth.

Jesus was likely born on a balmy night in September, when the air was clear and shepherds watched their sheep as they grazed on the pastoral land of Judea, just before the cold rainy season hit. So what does the Christmas season have to do with Jesus? Did Christians steal the thunder from pagan holidays?

From the beginning of the world, humans have celebrated time, and worshipped the sun, moon, and stars. It was 400 years after the birth of Christ when Christians took it upon themselves to fix His birth date around the winter solstice. In doing so, they took on many pagan celebrations. This doesn't sit well with some of today's Christian leaders who believe that Christmas (Christ Mass) came from the Roman Catholic Church, which got its ideas from terrors like King Pharaoh, and King Herod, who rejoiced over birthdays with all kinds of decadent celebrations. Instead of a birthday cake on a platter, those kings were reputed to have served the head of an enemy.

In his book *The Plain Truth about Christmas*, the late Herbert W. Armstrong tied all Christmas celebrations to paganism. On his television program his aged head tottered on bent shoulders as he, in a gravelly voice, denounced Christmas. He warned people not to teach their children myths. "Old Nick," he said, "is a term for the devil." Other Santa naysayers take it further by contending that because Satan and Santa have the same letters, they have the same meaning. I wonder how they would explain God and dog in that juggling context.

Armstrong saw holly, mistletoe, and the yule log as symbols that had nothing to do with Christianity. Yet, time and change bring new meanings. Today the mistletoe is a sign of peace and love as couples kiss beneath it. Holly is a sign of the cross and a harbinger of goodwill, and the yule log represents light and warmth.

Armstrong, the Puritans, and Uncle Fred didn't think much of bringing a tree into the house and decorating it, either.

"What would Christmas be without a Christmas tree?" I

exclaimed to Uncle Fred, a few months before he crossed over Jordan.

"Less pagan," was his retort. He believed he had the backing of the Bible according to Jeremiah 10:3, 4: "For the customs of the people are vain: for one cutteth a tree out of the forest. They deck it with silver and with gold. They fasten it with nails and with hammers that it move not." This was written in an era when trees were worshipped as gods. Christians esteem the tree as a symbol of the true Tree of Life, and regard its adornments as His light and beauty. The triangular shape represents Father, Son, and Holy Spirit, as it points upwards like a cathedral spire.

"It's ludicrous to drag a tree into the house and keep it there until half its needles fall off," Uncle Fred muttered as he pulled a stray hair from the tip of his nose.

"Mind now you don't badmouth Martin Luther, one of your heroes," I said, sending him scurrying to pull another hair from his nose.

Martin Luther, at the risk of being accused of losing his marbles, brought the tree inside. Neighbours saw this as odd. When he lit candles on the branches of the tree, they thought it not only odd but foolhardy. Luther didn't burn the tree or himself to a crisp, and soon the custom of bringing a tree indoors spread from Germany to England.

There are people who believe Mary's Boy Child should not be in Christmas, like the woman who stared at the manger in a store window and exclaimed, "What next? Now they're bringing religion into Christmas."

In many Canadian government offices and stores, employ-
ees are forbidden to display Christmas cards that depict the
Christ Child, or any notion connected with Him. Cashiers
and clerks have been ordered by store management not to
greet customers with "Merry Christmas," for fear it may
offend people of other faiths. A generic "Happy Holidays"
would be more likely to offend people who don't have holidays coming to them – happy or otherwise.

With the mixture of races and religions moving into the
mainstream of American and Canadian societies, Christians
like Armstrong may get their wish to have Christ taken out of
Christmas. Atheists and agnostics in the United States have
gone to court to have créches removed from public places.

It's unfortunate when Christmas is not seen as a time to
meet the spiritual and temporal needs of human nature in dis-
playing both spiritual and secular characteristics. In the midst
of political correctness, no one is offended by the secular
aspects of Christmas. Parents who do not want their children
to believe in what they deem to be "a fairy tale proclaiming
the virgin birth of the son of a mythical god" have no problem
enhancing their children's belief in the mythical Santa, who
has become for many the god of Christmas.

Amid the tinsel of Clausophobia, and the secularism of
the holidays, is a voice that whispers, "Yes, Virginia, there is
a Christ Child, and His gift is not something we hold in our
hands, but in our hearts – the gift of love."

Unlikely Mothers

For these two women the timing was all wrong – or was it?

Elizabeth stands in the doorway of her home. She wraps her robe tightly around her middle and presses her hand against her soft, sagging stomach. A sigh escapes her lips. She speaks her thoughts. "If only I could have a child! How I hoped – like Sarah! But Sarah had the promise of a son. I have only my prayers to give me hope. Now I have nothing to show for my life, not even any worthwhile work. It is different for Zachariah. He has his temple duties, and people around him to keep his mind off himself."

She sighs again, then turns from the doorway to go inside. Zachariah will soon be arriving for their evening meal.

Much later, after she and Zachariah have eaten, Elizabeth comes back and leans heavily against the doorpost. Her hand goes to the sash around her waist. She shakes her head and looks up toward heaven. "I never believed I would see Zachariah lost for words, but there he was, back from the temple with a strange look on his face. His hands were trembling when he handed me this note."

She pulls out a piece of parchment and smooths it out. Her old eyes bend close to it. She reads aloud the words her husband has written in his own hand: "Elizabeth, we are going to have a son. An angel came to me in the temple. He told me I would not be able to speak until after the birth of the child."

Elizabeth puts the note back in her sash. She smiles. "I laughed at first. Then I asked Zachariah how that could happen – he as old as he is. There was a new light in his eyes. I could almost see in his face the young man I married."

Elizabeth frowns and sits down on the stone steps. "My poor husband may have had a stroke and did not know what he was writing. Perhaps there will not be a child. In fact, the more I think about it, I believe it is the wrong time to bring a child into the world. It was fine in Sarah's day. But look at us. We are under the yoke of Rome, paying Rome's taxes. And I will never live to see a child raised. The psalmist wrote: 'The length of our days is seventy years. Any more means trouble and sorrow.'

"What if Zachariah's words are true? What will the neighbours think – our nosy neighbours and their noisy children? They will likely call me Johnny's granny. I cannot bear it."

Elizabeth hides away from everyone. Five months pass. Then one day as she looks toward the hills she sees a small figure on a donkey. She watches as it gets closer. It is Mary, her young cousin, from Nazareth. Her blue cloak and her sandals are dusty. Her cheeks are rosy, and her eyes bright under the dusty white shawl that falls around her head and down her waist. Elizabeth remembers when she was like Mary – young and full of hope and longings.

Mary slips from the donkey and calls to her cousin, "Peace be with you."

At the sound of Mary's voice, something happens inside Elizabeth. She gets her sign that all is well. At first, she is too stunned to speak. Then suddenly she shouts in triumph, "The Lord bless you, Mary. As soon as you spoke, the baby inside me jumped for joy. Now I feel young again and strong enough to bear this child. And you, Mary, are favoured above all women, for your body will cradle the Son of God."

Mary's soft, dark eyes fill with excitement. She must tell her cousin at once. "Gabriel came to me, Elizabeth! He told me you would bear a son also. I could not believe that an angel would come to me. People talked about seeing angels in the olden days, but I never thought it would happen now – and to me.

"He was robed in red and his wings were broad and bronzed, and tipped with gold. There was so much light around his head I could hardly look at him. When he spoke it was as if his voice filled the earth. Sensing my fear, he told me not to be afraid. I would bear the Son of God, and His kingdom would have no end. It didn't matter that I had never been with a man. The Holy Ghost would come upon me – and he did, Elizabeth! Suddenly it was as if my body became an empty vessel, and then I felt a warm presence filling it. I was overcome with joy. Now there is something inside me that makes me feel closer to Him. I no longer have to search outside myself. It is as if He is living inside me."

Elizabeth takes Mary's soft hand in her worn one. "When my baby is born I will lose the stigma of being barren; you will take on your stigma as people count the months. They may even count stones, and cast them. But the hand of God overrules both nature and man's cruelty. We need fear nothing."

Mary replies, "I did fear, at first. I thought of Joseph and what he would say. Would I lose him? Then as swiftly as those thoughts came, they were erased by faith. God filled me completely. It was as if I had become a part of Him, bearing His love to the whole world. I had to rush to you first, Elizabeth – though I didn't know why until I greeted you, and you responded."

"I am sure that Joseph has his sign by now," Elizabeth says. "God does not leave the message of His plans unfinished. You must stay a while. It is so lonely here looking out over the desert."

Mary stays for three months, and the two women prepare each other for their place in God's plan. Time moves swiftly. Mary kisses Elizabeth goodbye, and follows the road back to Nazareth, not knowing she will soon be back along the road to Bethlehem. She carries in her heart Elizabeth's words: "I have travelled far in my lifetime. I have feared and I have hoped, and I have passed uncertainty as if it were not there – and so will you."

Elizabeth watches her cousin disappear over the hills of Judea. Looking toward the desert, she imagines it alive with people coming to hear a voice – a voice in the wilderness. She recalls the words of Isaiah: "Make a road for the Lord through the wilderness; make Him a straight, smooth road through the desert. Fill the valleys: level the hills; straighten out the crooked paths and smooth off the rough spots in the road. The glory of the Lord will be seen by all people."

In time, Elizabeth gives birth to John. And on the Judean hills a chorus of angels announces a birth in a stable: "Glory to God in the highest, and on earth, peace and goodwill toward men."

Two thousand years later, we celebrate a time when youth, through Mary, and age, through Elizabeth, cradled Heaven's gifts. The two women journeyed through faith to give the world the fruits of promise.

Blue Slippers For Betty

Recently, on my Christmas rounds, I stopped to stare at two beautiful angels in a local craft store window. Then I saw the slippers! More than one pair this time! They were just like the ones my sister, Betty, had wanted so many years ago. My mind travelled back to when she and I were little girls swept into an idealist stream of thought that, with faith, anything is possible.

While reverently turning the pages of Eaton's Christmas catalogue, Betty had spied a pair of royal blue slippers trimmed with white fur and coloured beads. She was bent on having them for Christmas. On winter mornings, while our parents were still in bed, we had often danced our way, bare-footed and bone-chilled, into the kitchen. We cut off thick slices of loaf, caking them with pools of molasses and cold lumps of butter. Then we hurried back to the warmth of our bed.

"How are you going to get the blue slippers?" I asked Betty, one morning a week before Christmas, as we jumped into bed with our lassy bread.

"Baby Jesus will bring them," was her nonchalant reply, her cold feet bumping against mine.

Our father was a fisherman. If the summer catch was poor, there would be little money for needs and even less for wants. Our last resort was a "Dear Jesus" prayer mouthed in earnest while we knelt on a cold canvas mat by our bed. We didn't write "Dear Santa" letters. Our father thought little of a red-faced, jolly old pot-belly from the North Pole whose puffy red lips were plugged with a pipe when he wasn't mouthing the only three words he seemed to know: "Ho! Ho! Ho!" These were words any intelligent man would only utter if the trap door of his underwear were on fire.

No matter how little money there was, we always had a Christmas stocking. When it was opened, ambrosia cut through the cold morning air in mysterious tanginess from an orange, wrapped in its own tissue, and from an apple with points, one that when cut in two showed the star of Bethlehem. There would be grapes, a chocolate, and sweets. In the toe of the stocking would be either a Cracker Jack ring, a bracelet, or a toy watch.

When Betty ran into the kitchen that Christmas morning and hurried toward the coal stove, she didn't exclaim in surprise. She quickly dropped to the cold floor, the tail of her flannelette nightie under her knees, and reached to touch the slippers sitting there. She fitted them on her hands. Then she picked them up and ran back to our bed, pulling the bedclothes over her as she lay looking at the slippers on her hands, as if they were the open book of an answered prayer. They were the right colour, with white fur trim, and pretty Indian beads in front. I knew they would make a perfect fit. And they did!

Miles away, in Grand Falls, our cousins' father had a steady job in the Abitibi paper mill. It was the year the family sent us a care package of hand-me-downs. Among a pink training bra that my sister and I liked to model long before we were in training, and a black, satin garter belt – some earthly angel's solution to strangulating garters – lay Betty's Christmas gift. The pair of royal blue slippers must have arrived in Grand Falls from Eaton's catalogue the year before and were worn by a cousin whose feet had outgrown them.

My parents were not surprised. They believed that the pure and innocent faith of a child could mysteriously move humans to provide a practical solution. They taught us that miracles may come through a coincidence, a stroke of luck, or a prayer carried on the wings of a heavenly wind to earth-bound angels who deliver them. But they do come.

I don't recall what I received for Christmas that year. But I do remember how good those winter mornings were when my sister, fortified by her royal blue slippers, brought me a slice of lassy loaf while I kept the bed and my feet warm, taking for granted a Power higher than ourselves, one that holds the mysteries of life in all the seasons of our lives.

The Christmas Story: Past And Present

Six, five, four, three. . . . Children everywhere are counting the days, waiting, longing. Imagination is stretched to its limit. Nights disappear and mornings come holding too many tomorrows before that final day. Three, two, one . . .

Julie looks through her bedroom window. Her blue eyes glisten like turned-on Christmas bulbs as she watches the blinking multicolour lights shaping out houses all along her street. Her mother is waiting to read the Christmas story.

Julie finally turns from the window and jumps into bed. She nestles her head against her mother's shoulder and asks: "Mommy, were Joseph and Mary real?"

Elizabeth hesitates. Mary and Joseph have always seemed to be a sort of still life, a couple who never moved through the emotions of fear and doubt. Until now . . .

Centuries fall away. Mary sits brushing her shining mane of dark hair. Her senses tingle with a mingling of fear and excitement. The angel's annunciation is an echo, resounding over and over through her being. She will have a child – a child who will be the Son of God. A weakness sweeps through her. She drops her hairbrush and staggers to her pallet. What does it all mean? How can any woman carry within her body such a Being? And Joseph: how can she tell the man who has resisted every temptation to have her, believing that denial is as much a part of love as passion, that she is having a child, and not his?

Darkness hangs like a mantle around her as she hurries to Joseph's house. She draws him aside from the questioning eyes of his family. Her secret spills into his ears – drenching him and filling his insides like scalding liquid. Joseph would be thankful for deafness rather than to hear Mary's words. His suppressed passion has often tortured him, running through him like tongues of fire – and for this! His Mary would have a child by some other man. It is madness to believe that their God Jehovah has invaded Mary's body and planted an omnipotent seed in it. What has she done? If only she would tell him the truth: some man forced her.

"I must think, Mary," he says in a strained voice. He rushes away.

Joseph lies in the darkness, trying to fight off the ugly thoughts that leap into his head like snakes and wrap him in paralyzing fear. There comes a thought more hideous than the rest. Mary can be stoned for adultery if he rejects her. He falls asleep and dreams of Mary crouching on the ground, her young body defenseless against the onslaught of stones. He must defend her or Israel's unfair law will be swift and sure. A presence stirs through his dreams. A voice comes out of its depths, assuring him that Mary will indeed be the mother of God's Son. Doubt that has covered him lifts like a black fog; the truth warms and satisfies him. A deep joy runs through his senses. Mary has not betrayed his love, and now it rises whole inside of him. He must go to her and make her his wife . . .

Time regains its place and Elizabeth looks into her daughter's eyes. She answers with conviction, "Yes, Julie, Mary and Joseph were real."

Elizabeth's eyes take on a faraway look as her thoughts journey back. The decree has gone out that all the world should be taxed. Joseph is stunned to learn that he must leave Nazareth and go to Bethlehem to pay his taxes. Mary wants to go along, even though it is a long trip.

After demurring, Joseph decides that, if Mary should have the baby soon, then she must be with him. The donkey carrying Mary moves clumsily and often stumbles, slipping on stones as the couple moves slowly over the steep mountain trails. Mary cries out and Joseph asks anxiously, "Are you all right?"

Finally, Mary says in a faint voice, "You must hurry, Joseph." She tries to hold back the engulfing waves of pain, shivering as the cold east wind rakes her face. Soon they come upon lights poking through the gathering darkness; candles and lamps flicker from houses clustered together. Bethlehem stands upon the hill like a jewel set in the sky.

"You do believe, don't you, Joseph?" Mary's voice is

barely audible above the din of people crowding the narrow streets on their way to the village inn.

Joseph's answer is swift. "I should never have doubted you – not for a moment." He leads the donkey up to the inn door. White as porcelain, Mary's face breaks into a soft smile. Joseph relaxes. The innkeeper's eyes flicker over the couple. He turns away with a curt, "No room." Joseph tries to intercept him, but the innkeeper has no time . . .

"I would have given him my room, I would have, Daddy," a little boy insists, looking up from the Christmas story his father is reading. His eyes fill with tears. He forgets about the toys waiting under the Christmas tree. Instead, his thoughts travel to Bethlehem, where he watches Mary and Joseph turn away, having no place to lay Baby Jesus.

Suddenly the innkeeper's wife pushes past her husband's huge form. She notices Mary's swollen body under her heavy cloak and the lines of pain in her young face. "There's a stable nearby – warm with the bodies of animals. You'll be comfortable there," she promises.

The straw in the stable cushions Mary's body as she sinks gratefully into it. Rest is short! Pain fills her – tears at her insides like the claws of a demented animal. The innkeeper's wife brings a lamp, but Mary's world is in darkness, clamped under her tightly closed lids . . .

Christmas Eve is light: prisms of colour shimmering across the world. Mothers and fathers fill stockings, lift them swollen. There is promise. There is expectancy.

Joseph stands as still as a stone outside the stable, his eyes on stars blinking in the darkness. He does not see the wondrous star that will soon herald the birth of a King. There is aching and tearing in his own body as Mary's pain becomes his. Will the world remember; will it celebrate 2,000 years from now? Will it know that this Child was conceived out of God's love for man? Suddenly Mary's voice splits the silence. "Joseph! God! Why have you forsaken me?" Her cry is like a laceration in Joseph's flesh. Mary is the iron thrown in the fire to shape God's love into a human creation . . .

Children lie in their beds, refusing sleep. When it lies on their lids and forces them shut, they push at it. Sleep finally masters them and they drift away on its tides. There are no more tomorrows to restrain them from the wonder and the magic that is soon to come. Parents sleep away the exhaustion brought by Christmas preparations and the search through shopping malls for that perfect gift. The perfect gift is coming. Four, three, two hours . . .

Mary is borne away on tides that lift and drop her mercilessly. The soft voice of the innkeeper's wife is hard to hold onto. She lets the pain lift her; she cries for its mercy. Her body serves it. Suddenly there comes a sharp cry, as distinct as the brilliant star that pierces the night. It echoes through Bethlehem; its sound goes around the world. Love has come in infiniteness. Cradled in His mother's arms is God's greatest gift. For one moment the world pauses in obeisance.

Christmas morning comes! Children stir. Memory jolts

them awake. Stockings are emptied. Families gather around Christmas trees. The joy and love born in Bethlehem permeate the day like incense.

Turkeys sizzle in ovens. Families gather. The bond of love and friendship is sealed. There is no distance in time. Love synchronizes all generations and all peoples.

Like a silver thread woven through each Christmas, the love that was declared in a stable in Bethlehem will always find a special place in our hearts, for the love we share with those we love is an extension of God's love: the encompassing, priceless gift of Christmas.

The Gift Of Love

I won't need to dream about a white Christmas this year. Flurries tumble down on snow already caking the streets. I'm making my slippery run to the primary school for my seven-year-old's Christmas concert. He is (whether I believe it or not) going to be a Christmas angel. Not without some effort! The little imp will be masked in white crepe paper and trimmed with silver garland.

We pass houses outlined against the night by Christmas lights, each front door holding a live wreath with a big red bow. A new entrepreneur had made and sold these wreaths all around town. I look at Michael and ask, "What is Christmas all about?"

It is a needless question. He knows, doesn't he?

His answer is prompt, concrete. "It's about getting presents."

"Is that all?"

He shrugs.

Is it right that Michael thinks only of presents? I mull over his answer all through the children's renditions. We see Baby Jesus lullabied to sleep as shepherds holding staffs thump their way across the stage. Little wise men wearing tinfoil crowns follow, bringing gifts. It's a perfect night for the little angels to be singing "Silent Night."

There is not a sound in the crisp night air as we leave the school. Snowflakes are still falling, thickening the new blanket of snow.

I tuck Michael into bed. Fifteen minutes later, an urgent cry of "Mommy!" shatters the silent night. I hurry to push his door ajar, afraid he'd gotten a loose baby tooth stuck in his throat. His voice is low as he asks, "How many more hours before Christmas?"

He wants Christmas to come for one reason: presents.

I ask Michael an unfair question. "What if you had a dream, and in that dream Santa came and told you to make a choice between having us, or presents? What would you choose?"

Without hesitation he answers, "I'll have both."

His sister, who had a tiff with him earlier after he tied a limp string of spaghetti around a gift she was wrapping, calls out, "Let him decide between me and presents."

"That will be easy," he calls back.

I don't want to dampen his Christmas Spirit, such as it is, but I have to warn him that any little boy who would exchange his sister for presents doesn't really know the meaning of Christmas. "Why do you think the baby Jesus came?" I ask hopefully.

He shakes his head sideways. Just as I thought. Any sense of benevolence he had before Christmas has been dulled by the bright aspect of presents.

"The greatest gift," I tell him, "doesn't come wrapped in beautiful paper. The baby Jesus is both the gift and the giver. He comes to put love inside all of us. We all get the same amount. It's up to us how much we give to other people. Presents are things you play with, break, forget. Only love remains."

His sister calls from her room, "Mom, he doesn't understand any of that."

"I do," he calls back indignantly. "You don't know anything about love."

"Oh yeah? I know you can't wrap it."

"That's because it's already wrapped inside people's hearts," he retorts.

"You can show that you love other people by choosing one of your gifts to give to the little boy whose daddy left home," I suggest.

He promises to think about it, but only if his sister gives one of her gifts.

I close the door and leave him with his dreams. I can't expect him to understand love. We grown-ups haven't caught on yet. Like children, we so often demand the materialistic show of love with emphasis on the material rather than the love woven into it. Many adults make a choice between something they value and the thing that glitters for a time, and choose the fleeting gift over the lasting one.

Among the glitter of the gold and silver, we can teach our children to see beyond the wrappings, to look deep inside themselves for the gifts they have to give. We can teach them, not all in one year, but bit by bit, as the Christmas Spirit matures inside them, that love is the greatest gift to have and to give.

A Family's Christmas Gift

For most people, Christmas Eve is a time of great excitement. While parents busy themselves, children dance impatiently around the Christmas tree. However, in one home in 1983, a long-awaited Christmas gift arrived early. The home of Ted and Dorothy Kennedy and their children sits on the side of Harbour Hill overlooking Port de Grave Bay. Outside the house, softly falling snow frosted the beaded colours decorating the outdoor Christmas trees, creating the perfect setting for the scene inside. Three little girls – Natalie, Angela, Maryann – and their brother, Richard, couldn't take their eyes off the new addition to the family. Their youngest sister had finally come home after spending the first sixteen months of her life in hospital.

Jocelyn was born at St. Clair's Hospital July 21, 1982 with infantile polycystic kidneys: a disease which caused her kidneys to be covered with cysts and enlarged ten times the size of normal kidneys of children her age. Her kidneys pushing against other organs caused her to develop lung disease.

Without room to expand, her lungs did not reach their normal size. As a result, she developed respiratory problems. Her condition also caused high blood pressure. Doctors told the Kennedy family there was no hope for their baby. Most babies born with this disease die within three to twelve hours after birth. Ted and Dorothy knew only too well, through personal experience, what the doctors were saying. Elizabeth was born in 1979 with the same disease. She lived long enough to be given her name.

In one type of polycystic kidneys, the disease shows up later in life and isn't so severe. However, when both parents are carriers of the gene which causes this disease, the outcome is usually death in a short time. Statistically speaking, Jocelyn should not have been born with the disease; when both parents are carriers, there is only a one-in-four chance of passing it on to their children. The Kennedys' first four children were born healthy. Elizabeth was the fifth child. Jocelyn is the sixth and, according to her doctor's prediction, would die.

Jocelyn's mother, still mourning Elizabeth, was determined that her ill daughter would survive. She willed her to live from the moment she was transferred to the Janeway. Jocelyn was tube-fed and placed on a respirator. After she had survived her first day, finally passing urine, there was the slight chance for optimism.

In August, Jocelyn was sent to Sick Children's Hospital in Toronto Hospital in the hope a transplant would save her life.

Doctors decided that her kidney function was satisfactory. After a month there, she was taken off the respirator and sent back to the Janeway. However, because she was an active fighter, her oxygen supply was not adequate and she had to be put back on a respirator. When she experienced breathing difficulties, doctors did a tracheotomy on the four-month-old.

By January, Jocelyn wasn't doing so well, but her parents refused to give up hope that someday she'd be home with her family. In February she was taken off the respirator permanently. Then, almost a year to the day, she contracted a fever. Unable to bring it down, doctors placed her in isolation. While she was there, the feeding tube was removed from her nose, and oral feedings were started. Toward the end of November, the doctor removed the tube from her throat and, on December 2, she came home.

On Christmas Eve, Natalie, who was ten, was picking up Jocelyn and carrying her around as if she were the best Christmas doll in the world. The other children danced for their turn. The little girl with the big, wide eyes and dark, springy curls went into their arms without complaint, all the while looking as if she was wondering at the laughter, the chatter, and the coloured lights. Only now could she enjoy being touched and held without the pain of tubes and needles.

Two little girls knocked on the door. They entered the room shyly. One held out a present with both hands. "For Jocelyn," she said softly. Then the two girls hurried back outdoors. Throughout the evening, other gifts arrived. Even

Santa made an unexpected stop, just to visit Jocelyn. She was the community's child. Its people had been rooting for her ever since she was born. Having her home for Christmas lightened the hearts of many people who had nudged God with many prayers each time there was a crisis.

For Ted and Dorothy, the loss of their Christmas baby would always carry a keen pain, but they were thankful that their love, their church's faith, and the skill and constant care of the Janeway Hospital staff had helped Jocelyn – at that time, the only Newfoundland child to have survived infantile polycystic kidneys.

Little Jocelyn grew into a beautiful, energetic teenager. It was only then that she needed and received a kidney transplant. At her Christmas wedding when Jocelyn was twenty-three, I recounted the miraculous story I had written when she was a toddler. Jocelyn said, "While everyone else wiped tears from their eyes, I was smiling the whole time; I knew my story had a happy ending." For the coming years, her wedding guests will have an ornament to hang on their Christmas tree, in gold letters: Jonathan and Jocelyn, December 30, 2005.

Nighty-Night
Tuck-In Stories

Children of Christmas learn that the act of giving is a gift.

Christmas At The North Pole

Jeremy had never written a letter to Santa Claus. He had always counted on Santa to know what toys he wished for and to bring him some of them.

Today was different. Kristy had sneaked into his room and marked up his Narnia poster. He was feeling angry enough to grab her favourite doll, a Cabbage Patch Kid, and squash its fat cheeks, when his mother, hearing him yell, came to see what the fuss was about.

"A little pot sure gets hot," she sighed. Then she reminded Jeremy that he was seven and Kristy was only four. "We'll just have to get a lock for your door."

His father, who was in the living room reading the newspaper, called to him, "Come here, son. I've got the address where you can write Santa and ask him for another poster. The postal code is H0H 0H0, at guess where?"

"North Cold," Kristy sang out, pushing her head up under the paper.

That's it! thought Jeremy. *I'll run away to the North Pole.*

He got a pencil and some paper and started his letter. DEAR SANTA: When you come to my house this Christmas, don't bring me any toys. Instead, I'd like for you to take me back to the North Pole with you. You must have a large sack to carry all these toys, so when you've delivered the presents, please pick me up. I'll sit in your sack so I won't be any trouble. At the North Pole I'll help you make the toys (play with the toys, he meant), and I'll stay with you forever. LOVE, JEREMY.

He addressed the envelope and licked its edge. Then he sat on it to make sure it sealed while he daydreamed about life at the North Pole.

The next day, he realized that he'd forgotten to mail the letter, but he felt glad. He didn't really want to leave home. He went to find the letter. It was gone!

"You don't have to look for your letter," his mother smiled. He tried not to groan when she added, "I mailed it." He knew she wouldn't smile if she knew what was on the letter.

Jeremy found it hard to keep the tears back as the countdown to Christmas left fewer and fewer days. He would never forget his mother, with her blond hair tucked into a cap as she made cookies and mincemeat pies that seemed to bring Christmas right into the kitchen. He'd miss seeing his father with a towel slung over his shoulder as he washed and dried the dinner dishes. He would even miss Kristy and her little voice calling, "Germy." The North Pole seemed so far from home, so cold.

As Jeremy listened to all the Christmas plans, he got very heavy inside. On Christmas Eve, his father glanced across the room at him. "We must clean the chimney good," he said. Then he joked, "We wouldn't want Santa to turn into a black-beard."

Jeremy could just keep from crying as he hung his stocking on the mantel and went to bed early. He found himself sobbing against his pillow. If only he could say goodbye to everyone! But he couldn't tell anyone what he had done, or what Santa was going to do when he came. He wiped his eyes on his pyjamas sleeve and tried to think positive. If he worked hard as Santa's helper, perhaps Santa would put on an extra reindeer just to take him home next year. He tried to stay awake so he could tell Santa that his letter was a big mistake, and that he wrote it because he was angry at his little sister. But soon his eyes got heavy and he drifted . . .

Jeremy's eyes popped open and he found himself riding through the air, his arms wrapped tightly around a body that felt as soft as a stuffed toy bear. The fresh, crisp air had awakened him. He realized he was on his way to the North Pole. Ahead, he could see something that shone through the darkness like a red light bulb.

"Rudy's nose!" he exclaimed, getting excited. His eyes soon grew accustomed to the stars twinkling in the dark sky. In no time, it seemed, he was looking down on what appeared to be a floating castle. As Santa's reindeer and sleigh drew near, Jeremy thought, *This must be Santa's castle!* It sat on glittering ice. Conkerbells hanging from the eaves in rainbow colours glittered like rhinestones. His eyes were blinded by the most Christmasy sight he'd ever seen.

The reindeer and sleigh touched down gently, then slid across glittering snow crackling beneath them like broken glass.

A door to the ice castle was flung open, and a boy and a girl, dressed in red pyjamas, stood on the step. "Daddy, Daddy," they called in unison. "We heard the sleigh bells ringing."

Jeremy could not take his eyes off them. Seeing the boy was like looking into a mirror. He had Jeremy's thick, dark hair and brown eyes. The girl had blue eyes and bouncy curls just like Kristy's. A tall woman in a long red dress and white apron followed the children. *It must be Mrs. Claus,* Jeremy thought. She looked like Jeremy's mother and she sounded like her when she spoke. "You must be tired, Sandy, after being up all night."

Santa, who would have looked like Jeremy's Dad if he hadn't been wearing a soapsuds beard and mustache, let out a Ho!

Then Mrs. Claus spied Jeremy. "You've brought the boy." She sounded pleased. Her eyes looked him over from head to toe. Then she called, "Come along, young man. Good help is hard to come by these days. People don't believe that Santa needs extra help." She sighed. "Greed is keener than ever.

That means there are more and more toys to be made every year."

As Jeremy jumped from the sleigh, sharp ice stung his bare feet. The north cold went right through his pyjamas and slithered up and down his backbone. Mrs. Claus didn't seem to mind him dancing from foot to foot. "Bring Santa's sack inside," she told him, "and we'll see if there are any carrots for the reindeer. Then you can settle the animals in the stable."

Jeremy dragged Santa's sack to the castle and across the crystal floor inside, thinking that it wasn't very heavy.

The boy and girl let out squeals of delight. "Our presents," they chorused.

Jeremy opened the neck of the sack. He tipped it, and out fell carrots and cookies and a bottle.

"A bottle of Screech!" Mrs. Claus exclaimed, looking at Santa. Her mouth tightened. "That's what some people left you for your lunch! Why did you bring booze home?"

"Because," Santa chuckled, tickling her under the chin, "I couldn't drink and drive."

The boy and girl pounced on the cookies, then stopped, their faces mirroring disappointment. "No presents," they cried.

They looked at each other. Then they broke in again, "You brought us a brother, but no presents." They grabbed each other's hand and ran sobbing up the stairs.

"I left special presents for them in the workshop," Santa

explained to Mrs. Claus, "a Santa Kid for each of them – the first ones I've ever made."

"Well, they're not there. The shop is bare!" snapped Mrs. Claus.

"Perhaps the elves threw them in the sack; I forgot to tell them not to." Santa was apologetic.

Jeremy looked at them in amazement. They were just like a regular family, problems and all.

"I'll have a little snooze, then I'll see what we can do," Santa promised. He hugged Mrs. Claus. "You must not lose your Christmas spirit, my dear."

"It's okay," Jeremy said. "My mother often loses her Christmas spirit, but she always gets it back after Christmas."

Santa and Mrs. Claus smiled at each other as if Jeremy wasn't even there. Jeremy got the feeling that he was watching his mom and dad having one of their private moments. Suddenly he felt right at home.

"We'll go and tell the kids that their gifts will be waiting when they wake up," Mrs. Claus said softly. Then, hand in hand, Mr. and Mrs. Claus went up the stairs.

Mrs. Claus came down alone. "Santa," she explained, "is taking a short nap. We'll make the gifts and surprise him."

"We will!" exclaimed Jeremy.

"First," she said, taking the carrots that were in Santa's sack and putting them into Jeremy's hands, "you can feed the reindeer and settle them in the stable. Then we'll make two lookalike Santa Kids from Santa's pattern."

"But," Jeremy protested, "I thought Santa made all the toys by magic, and elves packed them."

Mrs. Claus pinched his cheeks so hard his eyes filled with tears. "Thought!" she sputtered. "You thought, but you're not thinking. Christmas doesn't just happen. Someone has to work hard. It is I who must work hard when Santa's gone."

"Gone!" Jeremy's eyes widened.

"I'm sure you've seen him sitting in village malls having his picture taken with children everywhere. That's where he earns his keep and ours. You can't live on bread if you have none," said Mrs. Claus. "We were fortunate to have my dad, Jack Frost, build us this home. You've heard of him, haven't you? He's an artist."

"Oh yes, ma'am." Jeremy's eyes lit up. "He paints silver ferns, horses' manes, and a whole lot of things on our windows when it's cold and –"

Mrs. Claus stopped him. "We have to get started." She passed him two Christmas stockings to pull on over his pyjamas legs. She smiled. "You'll have two stockings full this year, but it will be your own legs in them, and that's not a bad thing. You have to learn how to fill other people's stockings."

As they passed the stairs to go outdoors to Santa's workshop, Jeremy caught sight of two pairs of sad eyes peeping around the top of the stairs.

"I believe," said Jeremy, looking up into Mrs. Claus's face, "that Christmas should be everywhere."

"It never is," she said slowly. Then she pushed open the door.

Just as Jeremy stepped outside, a conkerbell broke off the ice castle and struck his head. He felt himself falling into a black pit . . .

Jeremy opened his eyes to find a cold finger on his nose. "Wake up, sleepyhead," Kristy yelled. She quickly dumped the contents of his Christmas stocking on the floor. *No carrots or cookies*, he thought. He sat up in bed, wondering why he should think about carrots or cookies.

There were lots of gifts under the tree. Jeremy opened his first present to find a Narnia poster. He shivered all through as he tore the paper off a Santa Kid. He gasped as Kristy tore the paper off an identical gift.

He let out a gasp, his eyes wide, as he remembered a little girl and boy who were still waiting for Christmas. He felt them near him – almost close enough to touch. Then he thought of other kids waiting for Christmas. Joby and Amelia, two little children up the street, would love a Santa Kid.

After all, he thought, *Santa needs all the help he can get.*

When Christmas Came
And Santa Claus Didn't

Santa knew something was terribly wrong the minute he dragged his tired body over the doorstep of his North Pole ice castle on Christmas morning. He dropped his red sack on the floor and straightened up to relieve his tired muscles. His nose hit an ice candle glittering in the morning air. It fell, breaking into slivers of sparkling crystal on the bright, diamond-hard floor of the castle. He wiped his sleeve across a cold nose; then he sniffed the air. The comforting aroma of Christmas breakfast was missing for the first time. His eyes lost their twinkle. "Oh! Oh! No!" he exclaimed.

He couldn't believe what he was seeing: Mrs. Claus dressed for travelling, her bags packed with their two children, Nicholas and Sandy, standing in them. "I'm leaving you," she said with a determined set to her jaw, as she zipped the cords under the children's arms, all the better to lift them into her sleigh. She dragged the bag to the door right in front of Santa and said, "I'm tired of being Mother Teresa of the North."

"B-but," Santa stammered, "we bring happiness!"

"To other people," she snapped, arching her silver eyebrows. "Christmas Eve is not a happy night for the children and me. We're home alone. The elves are conked out in the workshop after a hard year's work, while the reindeer are prancing through the skies hauling you in your sleigh. Our children have to wait for the milk and cookies left on Christmas Eve."

"I guess I have been neglecting you and the children, dear," Santa said in a voice that wasn't merry. "I'm not perfect."

"But the kids around the world think you are," sniffed Mrs. Claus, "and don't call me dear. A deer is a creature on four legs."

Nicholas and Sandy began to dance around. "We're going where we've never been before," said the children in unison.

"We'll be like other kids," declared Nicholas. "We don't want presents we've already seen – presents that are left in the bottom of your sack because they got broken."

"We'll live in a house made of wood or brick like everyone else, instead of in this ice house," Sandy added.

"The kids need to go to school with other kids," Mrs. Claus explained, "and I need friends."

"If you leave home," Santa said, in a voice no one could believe a *Ho! Ho! Ho!* ever came from, "what will you do?"

Smoothing back her white hair, Mrs. Claus tucked a strand into her bun; then she lifted a defiant apple cheek into the air. "I am experienced in designing toys and clothes, and I can market my special pot of jewelled candy. As Jack Frost's daughter I have the talent to do window etchings. I'm taking half the reindeer."

"You may as well take all the reindeer and leave me stranded," said Santa, disheartened at this turn of events. He sat on the ice staircase and sighed deeply.

"Why don't you retire?" Mrs. Claus asked candidly.

"You want me to retire from my work!" Santa exclaimed. "Would you tell God to retire?"

"Let's face it," said Mrs. Claus bluntly, "you're not God, though some people give you more attention than they give Him. Look at the letters you get from kids. It's 'gimme, gimme, gimme.' After the kids ask for everything they can think of, they remind you about the poor people. Then when Christmas comes, they tear away my beautiful artistic wrapping paper on one gift while looking for the next. But it's never enough. Your gifts are added to by parents and relatives trying to make greedy children happy. Do we ever hear from anyone after Christmas?"

Looking at Santa's downcast face, Mrs. Claus said grudgingly, "I'll stay with you – but only if you promise to relocate – if you promise to take the kids and move to sunnier climes. For years you've been promising them that we'd go to the beach. I want our children to see more than a sunrise on March 21 and a sunset on September 23. I want to see you in shorts instead of being all bundled up."

"I have a great idea!" beamed Santa. "We can make my sleigh trip on Christmas Eve a family affair. The younger reindeer are growing big. We can add an extra sleigh and get the work done faster. Then when we get back home I won't feel so tired. We can have a good Christmas Day together."

"I have a better idea," said Mrs. Claus. "We will all go next time, but we'll go on Christmas Day – not Christmas Eve – and we won't bring any gifts. If there are no gifts, then I'll be proved wrong."

Santa agreed reluctantly and Mrs. Claus and the children settled in for another year to daydream about how different their lives would be when Santa discovered that the children he was bringing gifts to didn't need them.

It was strange for Santa to stay home on Christmas Eve, but he did. He fidgeted a little and almost reached for the black pipe that he had given up smoking years ago. Then, putting aside thoughts of children who would be waiting for the sounds of sleigh bells, he and Mrs. Claus played games with Nicholas and Sandy. The children enjoyed the attention, and the special gifts their dad put under the silver tree for them.

The whole family, including the elves, got up early Christmas morning to harness the reindeer. Soon they were flying away from the North Pole, across the sky and down to the windows of homes, popping from house to house. The children were just getting up to see what Santa had brought them.

Santa's new team looked through the windows. They listened to starry-eyed children tell each other that they had heard sleigh bells in the night. "See!" Mrs. Claus told Santa. "Imagination will always be alive. If you leave the North Pole, that won't change."

A glass of milk and a plate of cookies left for Santa were still there. The sight brought only a shrug from children who figured that Santa had been full from mummering at other people's houses before he got to theirs. Just then a child looked at the card on his gift and read, "From Santa."

"Look Mommy!" he called. A pretty woman smiled. She had been giving Santa credit for gifts he hadn't brought since Thomas was born. That wouldn't change either.

Santa took in this scene with not even a *Ho! Ho! Ho!* Instead, when he and his entourage passed a food bank, he called, "Whoa! Whoa! Whoa!" to his reindeer. Then he did something he had never done before. He dropped in and picked up some treats for Nicholas's and Sandy's stockings, and snacks for the elves. It was the first time his children had their stockings filled with anything but their feet.

On the ride back home, Santa realized that he could leave the North Pole without causing hardship to other families. He quietly pondered his family's future. Then he gave them his special gift, announcing that they were going south for the summer.

Santa Claus decided to drop the reindeer off at the Salmonier Wildlife Reserve in Newfoundland and leave them there until the family found a new home. "The reindeer will enjoy time with other animals," said Santa. "While they're there, Dr. Goose can look up the nose of a certain reindeer and see why it's red."

Then, along with their elves, the Claus family taxied to Torbay Airport and boarded an airplane. The other passengers didn't wonder about them. Without their green garb, and pointed boots and hats, the elves looked like regular midgets. Santa and Mrs. Claus were disguised to look like everyone else. Santa had shaved his beard and packed away his red suit, black belt, and black boots. He had even discarded his red, fleece-lined longjohns. "They kept me warm and made me look fat and jolly, but where we're going," he declared, "I won't need to be kept warm and I won't need to be jolly."

The family settled in Havealot and Santa didn't utter "Ho! Ho! Ho!" – not even once. In fact, he became very serious. He found a job for the elves and himself in a toy factory. Mrs. Claus did silver etchings. She sold them to people who had never seen Jack Frost's work in this warm climate. Now these people were buying winter etchings of silver ferns and horses' manes to put on their windows all year.

When September came, Sandy and Nicholas went off to school. They were both excited until Sandy introduced herself as Sandy Claus. One child snickered, and then another, until the whole class was shaking with laughter. "You wouldn't be related to Santa, would you?" laughed a girl Sandy had become friends with after she'd met her on a beach during the summer.

Sandy's head dropped. She and Nicholas didn't fit in with the other children. She wanted to be back at the North Pole, where it was safe and she could be herself. Instead she stood up, lifted her head high, and announced, "This Christmas you won't get gifts from Santa, but I will."

The children stared at her. They weren't sure what she meant, but they weren't worried. They knew that Christmas would come with lots of gifts.

Mr. and Mrs. Claus decided to leave Havealot. They moved to a small town where poverty was vexing. It was a place where all the four seasons came in their time. It was a place where there had never been a sign of the fifth season, nor had anyone heard of it. The place was called Havenot.

Santa didn't mention Christmas, but he decided to build a factory making toys and other gifts. He and his elves cleared land for a farm. They bought cows, milked them and packaged the milk. They grew vegetables and fruit. They sent for their reindeer, who were probably missing them by now.

December came as usual, cold and white. On Christmas Eve, Santa took down a load of decorations he had stored in the attic. There were strings holding brightly coloured bulbs and ribbons that glittered like diamonds. Some looked as if they were made of gold and silver.

The people of Havenot watched as their strange neighbour strung lights across the eaves of his house.

"This fellow's mind has gone back to his childhood,"

remarked one man as he watched Santa and the children place toy snowmen and reindeer, and a fat man in a red suit on his lawn. No one asked him what he was doing. They didn't want to criticize or appear ignorant of the ways of foreigners. Then Santa went into the woods and came back home with a tree sticking out of his sleigh.

"He didn't even limb it for firewood before he brought it indoors," exclaimed one poor woman.

"He's sticking it up in his house!" another woman called. Soon the people saw the shadow of the tree standing in front of the Claus window. Santa winked and lights polka-dotted the night.

"The man has the missus and the children fancying up the tree as if it were a child they were dressing for a party," someone exclaimed. Next, the people saw their neighbour hide something in artistically designed coloured paper. He did that over and over until he fell asleep on the couch with a weary smile on his face.

"We can nab him and put him in the hospital to see if there's a chance of him getting right in his mind and acting like everyone else," said one fellow.

"Let's sleep on it," said another.

On Christmas morning, each family in Havenot found a pretty package in their house. At first, parents and their children sat around looking at their gifts and admiring the beautiful artwork that Mrs. Claus had painted of the North Pole. Finally, curiosity nudged them into pulling the wrapping aside very carefully so that they wouldn't tear the pretty paper. Then they cautiously lifted the pot of Mrs. Claus's jewelled candy.

The looks of pleasure on the children's faces rejuvenated the Santa family. They had a meeting and decided that Santa would go back to being Father Christmas, with the help of the whole family.

Santa immediately wrote a letter to the children of all the world: "Yes Virginia and Virgo, there's a Santa Claus, but he's like your dad. He has a boy and a girl like you, and like other working parents he's been too busy doing work people should be doing for themselves on the most special day of the year. He and his family have decided to spend their time helping the children of the world who are in want, children who have never heard of Father Christmas. You already have gifts given to you all year, and then more gifts on Christmas Day. Only parents who love you would be foolish enough to give credit to someone else for the gifts they work so hard to give. They do it to create magic. But love has its own magic. You don't need Santa. You can be Father Christmas."

"Mommy, a letter from Santa Claus!" one little girl exclaimed. "Can you believe it? He's not getting me anything this year."

"He's not?"

"No, it's right here."

"Well – I'll – I'll be . . ."

"You'll be what, Mommy?"

"I'll be, uh – I – I am surprised that Santa is a family man. I thought he was celibate."

"He does celebrate, Mommy. He celebrates Christmas, but from now on he's going to do it with his family and with poor people. He wants us to help."

A strange thing happened. Gifts arrived at Havenot town that weren't made at the North Pole. They were made in Japan, China, the United States, and Canada. Santa used his new factory to store the gifts and to sort everything out; he hired the poor people in Havenot to help.

Christmas came to a little boy sitting in the dust of a country where war and famine raged. Emli, who had never heard of Santa Claus, saw a shiny toy on the ground. He went to reach for it, then he fell back. His eyelashes batted weakly at a fly crawling on his face.

Evil men fighting each other in the hills and stealing from villagers across the plains saw a host of reindeer pulling a sleigh in the sky. Santa, dressed in silver armour, was holding a sword. It cut through the air as he urged his reindeer forward. The evil soldiers fled as if Michael, the avenging archangel, were on their tail.

Villagers felt safe. Mothers and fathers smiled through rivulets of tears as packages of food, grown on Santa's farm, floated gently to the earth. Sandy, Nicholas, and Santa's reindeer had made a special trip to the North Pole to harvest ice from huge bergs. They came back with their precious cargo.

Santa's helpers sealed cool, pure water in sacks made in Santa's factory. Children who had been crying from hunger and thirst now laughed with pleasure and satisfaction as the priceless gifts of food and water touched their lips.

Water touched Emli's hot lips. He sipped it and ate the food that lay in a Christmas stocking in his lap. Then, with all his strength, he reached for the shiny toy left for him. His hand touched it and he drew it to him. He had never felt joy like it before.

For the very first time, Christmas was everywhere.

Old Nart

It was almost Christmas, and the only present Mandy wanted was a doll. She pictured her eyes, shining like marbles, making a plopping sound inside her head as her eyelids, fringed by soft lashes, closed over them. It wasn't that she didn't miss her Annie doll, whose eyes were always open because they were painted on. But Annie was dead. She had swelled and cracked like a cake of hard bread in soak, after Mandy's brother, Jeff, threw her into a puddle of dirty brown water.

Mandy knew her father wasn't going to buy her a doll. He hadn't received a cent of unemployment money since he pulled up the boat last fall. A man down the coast, Eric Maley, was getting his cheques, and there wasn't a sound of help coming from the people in charge of unemployment payments. She couldn't depend on Santa either. Her father said that Santa Claus was some pagan invented by rich merchants to spoil children with promises their poor parents had to try and keep. Getting a doll was up to herself.

This was all Mandy could think about as she and Amy went

sliding on Kennedy Hill in the cove. The hill was like a slippery white boot. The girls raced right to the bottom, then coasted along the foot to the edge of the cliff, which happened to be right beside Old Nart's door. The old man had returned to the cove a few months earlier, after spending most of his life in Boston. There were whispers about him and voices like walls, discouraging the children of the cove from going near him.

In a snowbank just outside Old Nart's grey, two-storey house, Mandy spied the money. She reached for it, but Amy was quicker. She grabbed it; then she took off her cuffs so she could smooth out the bill. "There's number one and two zeros on it!" she gasped. "A hundred-dollar bill; I'm rich!"

"I saw it first," said Mandy, reaching for it again.

"You could see it all day," reasoned Amy, "but unless you got it in your hands, it's not yours." She pulled her cuff on over the money and grabbed the rope on her slide. Mandy watched as Amy started running. The red woollen coat that her mother had turned to hide its shabbiness slopped against her white fur-top boots.

An ache stirred in Mandy. That money could buy her a doll. "You'll have some Christmas," she called after Amy, "once your father gets his hands on the money. You'll be rolling across the floor on beer bottles, and your father's legs gone to jelly so he can't stand long enough to cut you a Christmas tree."

"My father won't see it." She kept on running and taunting. "Getters, keepers."

147

Mandy was lying on her bed facing the window, her mind on the money, when she saw Amy running across the icy road. She stopped below the window and called up, "The money, Mandy – it's funny money."

"Shush," said Mandy, pushing up her window and sticking out her head. "Open your hand for goodness' sake. The money won't fly away."

"See," said Amy breathlessly. "Queen Elizabeth is missing. Instead, there's a man on it. He's got woolly white hair and he looks as old as the hills. If I take the money down to the shop, Aunt Sara won't give me anything for it."

"That's what you get for being greedy," Mandy said with satisfaction. "That's George Washington, the first American president, or –" She peered uncertainly. "Maybe it's Benjamin Franklin. Never mind, it's money." Then it dawned on her that the money could belong to Old Nart.

Mandy had heard Aunt Sara talk about him coming into her shop and peeling a bill off a roll of money to buy cheese and bologna. She said he had old coins, too.

Aunt Edith, the oldest and sternest-looking woman in the cove, was always at the shop chawing about someone. She said Old Nart stole his brother's girl and took off to the United States. Now he was back, all grown over by a beard that hung under a mop of steel wool hair. "If it weren't for his cats," she declared, "birds would build a nest right on top of his head – and he's mare-browed, too."

"Mare-browed?" Mandy had ventured.

Aunt Edith had pushed a long finger under Mandy's chin and spoken in a stern voice. "That means his eyebrows meet, and anyone whose eyebrows meet is unlucky. Besides, he can put a bad spell on you."

When Mandy asked her mother about Old Nart she was told that he was just a poor old fellow the blessed Saviour died for.

"Then he doesn't sleep on a grapnel and –"

Her mother stopped her. "Pay no mind to the gossip trough. Some people have a tongue for prayers and one for prating, and the less they know about someone the more they got to say, especially if he's got the smell of a faraway place on him. That poor man's only sin is being smart enough to stay put until hunger drives him out for a bite."

Mandy's thoughts came back to the money as Amy reached up to pass her the crumpled bill. "Here," she said, "I'm going to wait for Santa to bring me a present." Amy believed Santa could get down her chimney, even if she didn't have a fireplace. He'd just let the air out of himself and squeeze through a crack or nail hole. Then he'd blow himself up again.

"You don't have to depend on Santa," Mandy insisted. "Stay right there." She ran across the hall into the cold front room. She pulled a small, wooden box from a shelf in the bookcase. Her father kept the graveyard box and the money in it that people donated to fix up graves in the spring. She counted eight dollars and forty-eight cents. That should be enough for two dolls. Then she put the hundred-dollar bill in the empty box. She brushed aside the guilt that hit her in the chest as she hurried out of the room.

"Only that much," exclaimed Amy in dismay.

"It's more than we had when we went sliding," reasoned Mandy, "and Dad's going to Bayview to buy some twine and nails. We can hide in the house on the truck. While he's in the shop, we can go to the drugstore and pick out our dolls."

When Amy wasn't greedy she was being a copycat, and the doll Mandy chose was the one Amy wanted. Luckily, the doll had a twin sister sitting right beside her. Leftover change was plopped down on the counter for some sweets from a big round bottle.

Mandy let out a sigh of relief when the girls reached the back of the truck. "I'm hiding my doll under the bed until Christmas," Amy whispered. "Then I'll tell Mom that Santa brought it. She won't know the difference."

The Sunday before Christmas came. Mandy sat in the Mission church trying to get her thoughts of Old Nart to go away. As was often the case, she was present in body but not in spirit until Pastor Butt, with a loud stamp of his feet as he was journeying through his sermon, brought her body and spirit back together. When he said that foolishness was bound up in a child, Mandy knew he was talking about her and her insides got heavier and heavier. She couldn't take the American money out of the box. Then it would be empty. She would have to give Old Nart her doll.

Amy said she wasn't going to give up her doll. "If you give up yours," she told Mandy, "you'd better go as a mummer, so the old man won't know who you are. When he opens the door, you can throw the doll in."

It was Christmas Eve before Mandy could talk herself into taking the doll to Old Nart. She'd already given her a name, and now she wrapped Angel inside her coat and sneaked out. The wind clipped her ears and pushed at her back, making her go so fast her legs got almost too tired to carry her body. Between the cold and the fright of having to face Old Nart, she was bivvering.

She knocked at the door and soon found herself facing a man she'd seen only from a distance. His eyebrows hung like mounds of snow over cliffs circling fierce-looking eyes, and she drew back.

"You be a mummer, I suppose," he snorted.

She pushed her bandana back over her head and stammered, "No – Sir, I'm Mandy, and I'm cold." She could see in around the door, where a brown Siamese cat sat glaring at her. Other cats lay asleep beside it.

"Don't mind the cats, girl. On winter nights they lie on me as pretty as a patchwork quilt and keep me warm. I hope they give out before I do, else they'll likely make a raid on the old bones. In you go, then, right over by the fireplace so you can dry that iron-rust hair of yours."

"It's not iron rust and it's not wet," said Mandy in an injured tone. "It's copper, like a new cent."

151

"That it is, then, and as long as a cat's tail."

Mandy looked around in astonishment. "It's clean in here." Her hand flew to her mouth. "Oh!"

"I see you've been hearing the rumours that have been flying like gulls." He took a pipe from the mantel and lit it. "I suppose you know about Elena," he said, noticing that Mandy's eyes had spied the painting of a young woman framed on the wall. "They say I stole her from my brother. It took my brother his whole lifetime to realize that I stole only Elena's heart. The rest was up to her. When he died and left me the house, I realized that, without the sounds of the sea in my ears, I was as good as deaf. I may not belong to the people in the cove, but I belong to the cove, the same as the land and the sea."

Mandy remembered that she had something belonging to him, and her story tumbled out. "It's Christmas tomorrow," she added, "and the new year is coming, and I can't go into the new year with the old year stuck in my conscience. Here, you can have my doll." She laid it on his arm and started for the door.

Old Nart caught hold of her hand and drew her back. He laid the doll back into her arms. "Dolls may keep little girls company," he said gently, "but an old man needs people. I didn't miss any money and what I don't miss I don't need. 'Tis a good thing you found it first." He chuckled and scratched his chin through a thicket of bushy hair. "If the wind had snatched it and taken it out to sea, the fish wouldn't have been as obliging as it was to Saint Peter."

Seeing the old man being so kind, Mandy reached into her pocket and pulled out a red tie. "My father never wore it," she explained. "It's a present. It doesn't look like you have any. Are you waiting for Christmas?"

"At my age, just being here is a present," he said, smiling.

"You can wear your tie to church," Mandy suggested.

He shook his head. "I don't believe in church."

"But you believe in life – your life and God's life. That's what it's about."

"The little bit of life that's in me isn't worth much, but I believe in something. I once saw someone bring down twenty-foot waves by making the sign of the cross."

Mandy looked at him doubtfully. "Waves always come down."

He took a puff on his pipe and squinted at her. "But they don't always stay down, not when there's a hearty storm on the go. Anyway, 'tis a fine name you got, Amanda: Latin for worthy of love, and virtuous in thought and deed. That you are, girl, but you had better be running home now, as fast as your legs can carry you."

It was stormy outside. Snow pellets hit Mandy's face like hailstones. She was getting tired of trying to push her way through the gale. If only she could tie herself to a gust of wind and be home! She was almost glad when she slipped and fell. Down she sank into a warm, feathery bed, feeling something like a skinned bird might feel at finding its feathers again. She closed her eyes and drifted with the snow.

The sound of sleigh bells brought her up out of a deep comfort. She couldn't believe what she was seeing: Santa, all covered in white like an angel, was lifting her into his sleigh. She fell sound asleep and didn't know anything until she awoke under a mound of bedclothes. She jumped at the sight of the bulging stocking at the foot of her bed. Christmas morning had come!

She was biting the points off her apple and sniffing its cold, sweet smell when her mother came into the room and put Angel in her arms. "I know what mischief you've been up to, and we'll talk about it after prayers," she warned.

Mandy was glad her mother had made her come to Christmas morning prayers when she saw Old Nart walk into the little Mission church. He sat right behind the pot-bellied stove. The old man was wearing the red tie, and suddenly he wasn't just a grey and white picture. He blended in with everyone.

The cove people were so surprised to see him at prayers that they all shook his hand when the service was over.

Mandy caught hold of his coat as he was leaving. He turned, and she looked up at him breathlessly. "I didn't believe in Santa Claus, but I saw him last night."

Old Nart winked, and a smile spread across Mandy's face. She winked right back.

Widdershins

It was Christmas Eve morning and Mandy looked up as Aunt Callie, tailed by Uncle Gus, pushed open the porch door and called, "Cheerio!" She eyed everyone sitting around the large wooden table and exclaimed, "Elizabeth, what a feast for sore eyes those children are!"

Mandy glanced at her mother's face. It looked flushed as she rushed around putting food on the table. Aunt Callie interrupted her with a big squeeze. Then in a plaintive tone she asked, "Don't you think, Elizabeth, you should share at Christmas? Let me take one of the children for a few days." She looked toward Jeff expectantly. Jeff, who was now fifteen and in no mood to be shared, turned away. Michael was ten and he, too, was in no mood to spend Christmas at Smith's Point. Taylor, seven, and four-year-old Timmy were more than Aunt Callie could handle. Her eyes swivelled to Mandy.

"Well," Elizabeth said, without much heart, "if Mandy wants to spend Christmas with you . . ." Her voice trailed off.

It wasn't what Mandy wanted. Christmas meant being at

home with the other children, taking part in squeals and laughter as stockings were emptied, and red and green tissue paper was torn off mysterious-looking presents. How could a visit to Aunt Callie's compare with that? There would be no tree, just strangers straggling in for their glasses of grog. She'd be expected to sit on the settee in a large kitchen and keep quiet while strangers scrutinized her and discussed whose nose and eyes she might have come by.

She wanted to stick out her bottom lip and tell everyone, "I won't go." The words were almost to the surface when the Christmas spirit tapped her conscience. She found herself thinking there would be no Christmas if people didn't share. *I suppose*, she thought reluctantly, *I could be a borrowed gift – one that is returned once Christmas is over*.

Mandy went to pack. She stopped halfway through. The thought of spending Christmas at Smith's Point sent a shudder of loneliness through her. She felt as if the sea just out from her aunt's and uncle's house was all around her – as dark as the inside of a wolf's mouth, the wind around Smith's Point as lonely as a wolf's howl. If only it were summertime, when sunshine and gentle winds made the place friendly. She liked to stand on the upstairs landing and look down over the cliffs of land rising high above the waters. She'd watch the sea beat itself upon the rocks in an explosion of white spray, then fall, to be enveloped again by its dark self. On a clear day she could look across to the point of land jutting out into the sea and take comfort that it held her house, even if it was on the far side and out of sight. Mandy shook her head as if to knock some sense into it. After all, she was twelve – a proper age to begin thinking about someone other than herself.

Mandy's mother came through the hall and stood in the bedroom doorway. "You be good while you're gone," she said, pushing her hands down over her middle as if to flatten her large stomach. A frown crossed her face. "And stay clear of your uncle Gus's brother, Old Josh."

As Mandy was leaving her room, she stopped at the sound of her parents' voices in the hall. Her mother's voice carried an edge of worry. "I hope Mandy won't be afraid of the drunks Gus brings home. Old Josh will probably be around sniffing for a bellyful of liquor, while his woman and that little girl of his starve in the paper shack he's hauled over their heads."

Her father sighed heavily. He muttered, "After what happened to the boy, Josh can be called nothing but a killer." Her parents' voices turned to lighter conversation as Mandy came into the hall.

It was a half-hour's ride to Aunt Callie's and Uncle Gus's, along the shore, then up over hills that dipped into valleys; the final ten minutes were spent following a road that edged the high cliffs like a pencil mark. Mandy shuddered as she remembered that on a dark night last winter a man had gone over the cliffs and died.

The two-storey house, with a roof like a witch's hat, came in view. Soon Mandy was inside the cold house. It seemed empty, with only the voices the three of them brought into it. There was not even a radio to carry *A Christmas Carol*, a story Mandy was used to listening to every Christmas Eve night.

Once fire filled the black stove, the air began to warm up. Soon water in the kettle began to gallop and spout, tissing as beads of it popped along the damper. Mandy began to feel more at home as heat seeped into her bones. She went to read Christmas cards strung across the wall on red twine. She pressed her fingers down on those cards puffed with powder under silk bells tied with ribbons; her fingertips ran along the cards coated in glitter.

Aunt Callie called her away from the cards to sit for a mug-up of milky tea and bread with homemade partridge-berry jam and Nestle's tin cream. After they had eaten, Mandy was left to wash the dishes in the pantry while her aunt took down her cap. She pushed her frizzed, grey hair up under its edge and began to mix some molasses buns. Now that she was past seventy, her cheeks were becoming more and more like shrivelled potato skin, but her eyes were bright, as if they were sitting in water.

"Are you making buns for company?" asked Mandy.

"Yes, child, I expects quality every time I leaves the cover off the teapot." Aunt Callie called company "quality." When she received quality, expected or unexpected, she served her best food on her good dishes, spread on her finest tablecloths. They were made from flour sacks and bleached to a dazzling whiteness. Each cloth was embroidered from corner to corner with flowers and fancy edging.

"Praise be!" Aunt Callie said. "There's Gus's buddies coming for their swigs now. That's the rigmarole on Christmas Eve – not like at your house, where your father wouldn't put a stain of liquor to his lips."

Mandy skittered out of the pantry and through the kitchen to the parlour, just past the foot of the stairs to the bedrooms. She closed the door and settled in Aunt Callie's big chair, hoping the roars and the laughter wouldn't come any closer. Suddenly the door creaked open. A man who looked a lot younger than her uncle came into the room. "I heard tell of you," he said boldly. "You're the girl with the upturned nose and the horse's mane of hair."

Mandy pressed against the back of the chair as he came closer, his face flushed and his eyes bright. There was a strong smell on his breath that reminded her of the hops her aunt used to help her bread dough rise.

"Would you like some money?" the man asked, his breath hot against Mandy's face. She didn't answer and he dropped some coppers into her lap. "I could spit on them for good luck." He grinned.

Mandy tried to answer indignantly, but her voice came in a hoarse whisper. "No, thank you."

He laughed. Then he stooped down and pushed his hand under the coins in her lap. Mandy made a sudden movement to stand, and the man tipped back on his heels. The coppers fell to the floor, some of them standing on end in the braided mat. There was a sound outside the door, and the stranger stood up. He hurried over to the mantel, where he leaned whistling and pretending to look at her aunt's and uncle's wedding snap. Mandy's shoulders sagged in relief when Aunt Callie came into the room. Her voice was stern. "Come along, young man – out among your own crowd."

Mandy was glad when the porch door slammed for the last time and the house settled down. Then there came the sound of the porch door being unlatched. "Company again!" Mandy exclaimed in dismay.

"I've had company," Aunt Callie sniffed, "and a fine lot they were. They left the house loosened up like rag dolls. No, that's Bertha from next door. I was looking out the pantry window and I saw her coming down the lane."

"Nice clear afternoon for Christmas Eve," called Bertha, sticking her head in around the door facing. "Old Josh is in his drinking habit. I saw him trailing all over the road. I heard he's beating Jane again, and only six months after poor little Joey died. 'Tis an awful sight to see her with black eyes against that white drawn skin of hers." Bertha sniffed and her lip curled up toward her nose. She pushed a heavy hand against it; then she rubbed her hand down her bumpy hip. "I got a cold, I have."

"Then don't do what Gus did," warned Aunt Callie. "He sniffed hyssop salts up his nose and emptied his head of everything – even his brains, I declare."

"I'm not that drastic," snorted Bertha. She pulled her bulky body over to the window. "There he goes, Old Josh, off to houses around the place smelling for a grog. He won't know he has a soul when he's finished, and the little one and that woman of his won't know it's Christmas. I better get on over to the house and lock the door, just in case he shows up."

"A beggar's claptrap, that's what she is," Aunt Callie said, once Bertha's back was in the distance, "always minding other people's business."

"Salt herring," Uncle Gus said with relish, as he lifted the cover off the steaming pot. He sniffed the steam. "Ha – 'tis better than a rock in a pot for Christmas Eve." He took hold of Mandy's hair. "What are you expecting from Sandy Claus?"

"Nothing, Uncle," she answered, pulling her hair out of his hand.

"Nothing!" He raised his voice. "That's a hole with no sides. We won't have that here."

Aunt Callie's eyes took on a thoughtful look. She left off setting the table, and stood for a while with her knuckles on her broad hips, making her arms stick out like handles on a jug. "I think," she said, with a nod toward Mandy, "we'll dodge down to the shop."

"Will we see Alice?" Mandy asked.

"Alice?"

"Yes. Old Josh's little girl."

Uncle Gus's eyebrows lifted as he answered. "Since their

house burned down, she lives in a brown house built outdoors under Penny's Hill."

"Knock off your foolishness," Aunt Callie jawed him, "and don't stretch your suspenders."

Uncle Gus's molasses-warm eyes turned muddy brown. "Hush, woman! If I wanted to get henpecked I'd go down to the henhouse." He pulled a block of Lady Twist Tobacco from his pocket and twisted off a piece with his teeth.

Mandy could have laughed at him chewing on his cud and running his tanned, hairy hand over the top of his head, where sparse hair sticking off made his brown head look like a coconut. But she'd rather die than have her uncle squirt his baccy juice over her clean dress.

Mandy followed her aunt to get their coats and boots.

"Do you think we could buy some Christmas apples, the ones with points?" asked Mandy, as they trudged through the deep snow.

"Indeed we can. I've a few cents for that."

"Right in the centre is the star of Bethlehem," Mandy said excitedly.

"That's the ones," her aunt replied, "and I've saved enough money to buy a duck for Christmas dinner. We'll have Alice and her mother up – Josh, too, if he can put one foot in front of the other. In some ways, that man is like his mother. God rest her soul – if He can. She was a bad one. Living with her in this house was like having one foot in hell, which is where she must have found her feet when she was dying. She sat in her rocking chair and asked for water. Before I could get the tumbler to her lips, she was gone. It was a wonderful thing. I no longer needed eyes in the back of my head for fear there would be a pot of scalding water thrown at me. 'Tis Christmas, and now I'm being the claptrap."

Aunt Callie pushed open the big, wooden door to the shop. A brass bell above the door let out a loud peal. A small woman behind the counter smiled and greeted them. "A Christmas box on you and yours."

"And to you and yours," Aunt Callie answered.

Mandy eyed a big, round bottle of hard knobs on the counter. While her aunt picked out some apples and a large duck, she took the five coppers her mother had given her and asked for five cents' worth of sweets. She turned quickly when she heard her aunt say, "Hello, Alice, how's your mother?" Alice's thin, yellow hair hung in strings around her pale face and across the collar of a blue coat that had been turned to hide the faded colour. Mandy remembered seeing Alice once when she and Aunt Callie had walked to Long Cove. The family had lived there before their house burned.

Alice answered timidly. "She's okay, Aunt."

"Only a few hours until Christmas," Mandy said, smiling.

"I can count forever," Alice answered sadly, her eyes like blue buttons in ragged, black-stitched buttonholes.

"But, it's tomorrow." Mandy's voice rose with excitement.

Alice shook her head. Tangled hair fell into her eyes as she bent her head, making her look like a rag-moll.

"It will come, if you believe," Mandy told her.

Alice lifted her head. A flicker of hope came into her eyes. Then, just as quickly, it died.

Aunt Callie's voice was brisk. "Come along, Mandy." She turned back to Alice. "Tell your mother I'm expecting all of you for Christmas dinner."

"Yes, Aunt." Alice's voice quavered as if she was uncertain.

As Mandy and Aunt Callie walked home, the falling snow enclosed them like the tossed flakes in a water globe. Just below Aunt Callie's house, Mandy noticed a dark patch on the snow. The evening was darkening, but her aunt knew what it was right away.

"That," said Aunt Callie in an indignant voice, "is Josh. He's done it again. Not only does he not keep Christmas, he does his best to try to steal it from everyone else. I'll ask Gus to help him get to the house; otherwise, he'll perish. We'll stretch him on the daybed and let him sleep off the only Christmas spirits he knows anything about. If he comes to and acts up, Gus will put a fist to his jaw."

Mandy had never seen anyone drunk before. The thought of being in a house with a drunk man made her as skittish as a wild horse. She started to run past the curled-up figure, past her aunt's house, and across the lane to Bertha's. She paid no heed to her aunt's call to wait. The sound of running brought Bertha to the door. She opened it, and Mandy fell into her arms panting, "There's a man – Old Josh – he's coming to Aunt Callie's house."

"You're right in feeling scared," said Bertha, drawing her

inside. "Drunks," she continued, with a gleam in her eye, "are the only spirits of Christmas – take my word. I've had strangers, that I'd never before laid eyes on, pounding the door. Like mummers, they were, huffing to get in."

Mandy and Bertha watched from behind the curtains as Gus dragged his brother toward the house. Mandy's voice quavered. "I can't go out there; he'll grab me."

"He's done some terrible things," said Bertha. "I heard your uncle say, 'Josh, you got it coming to you. Retribution, it's called; it's on the way.' Billy, the oldest, moved out last year. Every now and then he fires a rock through the window, hoping to hit the old man."

"That's awful!" Mandy exclaimed.

"It seems that way, but Billy learned evil from his father. He pushed him down the stairs one night and told him he hoped he'd never walk again. Other times, he'd come home late at night and dribble over the children's beds. Then he'd push them out of bed and order them out the door, sometimes on the wildest winter nights. After that, he'd crawl into bed beside Jane and sleep like a baby. If he has a conscience, no one has ever seen a sign of it – unless 'tis the devil, and he's taken what he could get."

Bertha lowered her face, making her double chin triple against her fat neck. "When he's drunk, 'tis as if the devil comes to life in him as plain as day."

Mandy stared at Bertha, her eyes brimming with tears. "Why didn't Alice's mother stop him?"

"She tried – but she was no match for Josh's fists. One time, he knocked her out with a trotter bone. Your aunt always took Joey in, and Alice, too, when she didn't find some place to hide. I minds one time when your aunt and uncle were away. Joey came knocking on my door. He was a small frame in his one-piece underwear, and he stood on my step in his bare feet jumping from foot to foot and shivering like a little lamb. I took him in for the night. Then last January he took with meningitis and – only God knows what else. By the time he died in June, he was curled up something terrible; his little hands were bent like lobster tails. He was thirteen, an unlucky number for him. Old Josh sat at the wake with his elbows on his knees and the backs of his hands under his chin. I couldn't help speaking my mind. I asked him if he remembers all the nights he threw Billy out the door. Then I said, 'now he's outdoors for good.' I had to get up and leave for fear he'd strike me, but like any decent soul would, I got my word in. Since then – as far as I know – Alice doesn't get disturbed."

Mandy jumped at the sound of a knock at the door. The latch lifted, the door opened, and her uncle came in. "Come on," he said briskly, "home with you." He grabbed her hand and held it tight. Mandy went without a word.

She didn't speak as they went down the lane, and once she was inside the porch she dropped back behind her uncle. Fear tightened around her spine like a fist when she looked across to the daybed and saw a man stretched out, and snoring loudly, his mouth open like a black hole. His face, under a head of hair like black sheep's wool, looked yellow and cracked, as if an earthquake had shaken it.

"Hurry, child," said Aunt Callie, "up to bed with you, so you can get an early start on Christmas Day."

"I can't – Aunt – I can't pass him." Her voice faltered.

Aunt Callie held out her hand, and Mandy took it. She held herself tight against her aunt's body, away from the man on the daybed. Just as they passed him, he let out a snore that almost dropped Mandy to her knees. Fear bit into her backbone and she ran into the hall. She caught hold of the stair railing, hitching her toes in the metal clips that nailed the stair canvas.

"That man can't hurt you," Aunt Callie called.

"But Bertha said –"

"Bertha!" Her aunt shook her head. "I already told you she's a tongue-wagger."

"Are they true, Aunt Callie – all those terrible things?" asked Mandy, once she was on the stair landing.

"'Tis true, Lawd Gawd," her uncle muttered heavily as he came up the stairs. "If I let myself think about it, I'd heave his carcass out the door and let him bide to freeze."

"Stop trembling, child." Aunt Callie's voice was gentle. "No one should be afraid on Christmas Eve." She drew Mandy against her warm, hot-water-bottle softness. Then she took her hand and led her over to sit on the wooden trunk under the window. "Let me tell you about Josh. He was about your age when it happened."

"It happened?" Mandy looked at her aunt and frowned.

"Josh had stayed too long at his cousin's house. It was getting dark, and he decided to take a shortcut across the marsh. According to him, an old woman with an Aladdin's lamp caught hold of his hand. She didn't let go until they had crossed the marsh; then she disappeared. When Josh got home he was in a state of shock. The fright must have turned his blood, because he swelled up like a poisoned rat. His mother had to press down his tongue to get in water. When the old doctor came he told Gus, who was a little older than Josh, to run quick and get some twigs. The doctor twisted the twigs into a cross and then made the sign of the cross over Josh. He asked what time the spell had taken him. Then he shook the clock and did widdershins."

"Widdershins?" Mandy screwed up her face. "What's that?"

Aunt Callie explained. "The doctor turned back the hands of the clock to the time Josh got the fright; then he wound it contrariwise until the spring broke. That was the doctor's way of breaking the spell. 'Twas a lovely grandfather clock, but it never told the time again. It was kicked around outdoors for a long time. The doctor left a flask of whisky. He told Josh's mother to keep a flask in his pocket every day, so his nerve would get strong. The doctor didn't say when she could stop, and she didn't ask. Months went by, then years, and Josh was still nipping at the bottle." Aunt Callie's eyes got angry-looking when she continued. "He got frightened by one spirit, and he ended up with another one fixed to him for life."

"Whose fault is it?" asked Mandy.

Her aunt sighed. "The world isn't perfect, child. In a way, Josh is only as bad as he was made. We have to do our bit to help everyone who suffers. That's why your uncle, for all his barking about Josh, does what he can to help out."

Aunt Callie raised an eyebrow in Uncle Gus's direction. He shrugged, and reminded her that there was a surprise for Mandy down in the parlour.

Mandy followed her aunt back downstairs, with Uncle Gus coming behind. She peeped cautiously into the room. "A Christmas tree," she whispered. Then her mouth dropped open. "It's bare."

"Just as God made it," said Aunt Callie with a firm mouth, "not fancied up, or false."

Uncle Gus snorted. "Now, woman, don't confuse the child. God made you bare, but you wouldn't be caught in the open that way. A few cranberries on some Christmas twine would brighten the tree. You could always make a dish of jam from the berries afterwards."

Aunt Callie ignored his suggestion. Her eyes flashed over his remarks about her. "Your mind, Gus, 'tis always in the devil's workshop."

Across the hall, Josh let out a snore. Mandy turned in fright and started back up the stairs. Her aunt called after her, "These are wonderful times, my dear. When I was a girl, things were bad. I was a servant girl at your age – up at four in the morning – drawing a turn of water from the well, two buckets on a hoop. Yoked, I was. I fell asleep more than once with my hands in the bread dough." She flapped her hand as if to shoo Mandy off to bed. "Never mind. That's all behind."

Mandy burrowed deep into the feather bed, letting her feet rest on the round, smooth rock that her aunt had warmed and wrapped in flannelette. Her thoughts went out like a light, and she slept.

She awoke suddenly, something touching her senses. Excitement came like a ripple widening inside of her. She sat up quickly, pushing the fat feather pillow behind her back, then reached toward the stuffed wool vamp lying across the foot of her bed. The first thing her hand touched was an apple. She rubbed it against her nightie to make it shine, then she bit off one point, drawing the sweet Christmasy scent up her nose. Then she laid it aside and reached to take out an orange wrapped in its own tissue paper. She tipped the vamp and out fell sweets wrapped in shiny paper. Her Christmas box lay at the foot of the bed. She reached for it, taking her time untying the green twine holding her present wrapped in red tissue paper. She closed her eyes so she could better hear the mysterious rustle of the paper as she unfolded it. She slowly opened her eyes. They widened at the sight of a pretty cotton apron with a frilly bib. There were pictures of kittens all over it. *Alice would love this Christmas box, and anyone can be Santa Claus – a man, a woman.* "Even me!" she exclaimed.

Mandy jumped out of bed and pulled on her brown stockings. She shivered her way into her red wool dress. Then she stood on the hooked mat and did her best to rewrap the present. She put the apple and some sweets into her pocket. The window was a silver plate of designs in wings and horses' manes – and a silver tree, through which she blew a black hole. She looked through it. Her mouth opened at the sight of snow glittering in sunlight. She could see conkerbells, or ice candles, as her aunt called them, hanging from the eaves of Bertha's house. Tree branches held up fingers in silver gloves.

She turned from the window and tiptoed out to the landing. Silence was all around, like a breath held in. She tried not to think of Josh as she slid her hands carefully down the stair railing, keeping the weight off her feet so the stairs wouldn't creak. She turned her face away as she pushed open the door and passed Josh, her heart racing. He let out a loud snore and she jumped in fright. She hurried into the pantry. There she took a knife and cut her apple in half, hoping that Alice would see the star of Bethlehem in the centre. She wrapped the half-apple in a flour bag cloth and pushed it back into her pocket. She wouldn't look at Josh as she went into the hall to get her coat.

Mandy walked across the crunchy snow in her white fur-top boots. Blossoms of snow began to fall thick and fast, covering her hair like a lace scarf. It was the most beautiful Christmas morning world she had ever walked into.

This must be the house Alice is living in now, thought Mandy, coming to an old brown bungalow. She reached up and lifted the latch on the grey matchbox door. She pushed it open, holding her breath for fear its hinges would squeak. There were no sounds, only a cold emptiness as she went through the porch into the big kitchen. Alice lay asleep on the daybed under old coats and a quilt like the one on the bed Mandy was sleeping in. Her hand was under her chin. Mandy placed the present, the apple, and sweets on the bed, noticing that the contents in the chamber pot by the bed were frozen solid.

Mandy hurried back to her aunt's house. This time she forced herself to stop and stare at Josh. He looked, as her aunt would say, like a poor mortal rather than an evil man. To prove she didn't have to be afraid, she reached out a trembling hand and gingerly touched a nose that was sprouting hairs. *Probably fertilized by the booze*, she thought. His eyelids lifted slightly; then they dropped again. "Merry Christmas," she said hoarsely. Then she turned and crept upstairs and into bed to wait for the stove fire to be lit.

"Do you like your apron?" Aunt Callie asked when she came downstairs for breakfast.

"Yes," answered Mandy, "it was beautiful."

"Was? Where is it?"

"I gave it away."

"You gave it away?"

"Yes, Aunt – to Alice. I went over this morning."

"Oh." Aunt Callie's eyebrows lifted, and her eyes looked

thoughtful as she turned to crack two brown-shelled eggs into the frying pan. "Why?"

"Because, well . . ." She went on in a rush. "My dress doesn't get dirty if I'm careful. I don't really need it."

"And Alice needs it?" her aunt asked gently.

"I don't know, Aunt Callie." Mandy moved in front of her, and said with conviction, "She needs Christmas."

Her aunt smiled and said quietly, "Since Alice already has her Christmas box, the one under the tree must be yours."

Mandy went into the parlour and lifted the present from under the tree. She slipped off the green twine and opened the red tissue paper. She smoothed out her apron so she could see the kittens. *I guess*, thought Mandy, sitting in front of the tree, *Christmas away from home isn't so bad, not when you give away your present and get back one exactly like it.*

Christmas At The
Grenfell Orphanage 1923

An excerpt from *Far from Home*

A few more days of the blistering voices of grown-ups splashing vinegar into the cuts of children's lives and it will be Christmas.

Clarissa looked up from the pages of *Just Looking at You*, and the complaint of the book's forlorn heroine. "That sounds like this orphanage," she muttered.

The eve of Christmas slipped in through a dark morning and opened up into a crystal-white day. The scent of Christmases past seemed to waft against Clarissa's nose; the gaiety of the season came like a red candle, its flame a dancing ballerina. She felt her insides liven in the shining hope of Christmas. *Even miserable Miss Elizabeth is going to enjoy Christmas; she won't be able to help herself,* Clarissa thought as she made her way to the dining room.

"Chew, chew, don't talk." Today Miss Elizabeth's voice

was gentle as she came into the dining room, where the children's whispers had burst into chatter. The children looked toward her as her thin lips opened into a smile – a Christmas surprise.

Later, when the children were dismissed, they scattered into the hall. The mistress's pleasant look disappeared into a frown at the sight of what she called hijinking conduct by boys wrestling on the floor. She tutted, "You boys are bent on hurling the Christmas spirit out the window." Afraid that the dreaded words "no lunch and no supper" would fall on their ears, the boys got up and scampered up the stairs.

Still, Christmas is the best of times, even better than birthdays, because a glad spirit is in so many people at the same time, Clarissa thought as she stood on the orphanage steps after lunch. *Everyone's thoughts are strung together in the hope of getting a Christmas box that will make them forget all the bad things that ever happened to them.* She would be able to forget the housemothers' and mistresses' scoldings, the orphans' taunts, and her uncertainty about ever leaving the orphanage, if there was a present from her real family. Her heart somersaulted in anticipation.

From where she was standing, Clarissa could see the Grenfell Hospital. Against its front walls, on packed snow, harbour dogs lay with their tails curled over their noses. The dogs looked up at the windows now and then, as if searching for a familiar face and a treat. A guarded look crossed their faces and their ears stood up straight when they heard the squeals of children and the howls of huskies mingling in the afternoon air. They knew what would happen to them if a temperamental husky got loose from its traces.

Dr. Grenfell had given the orphanage boys a husky dog team. Now Jakot, Peter, and other older boys were on their way up Fox Farm Hill to cut a tree and greens to decorate the orphanage. The huskies bristled and lifted their heads, howling like wolves as they pulled the sleds past barking harbour dogs. Jakot, the driver, swung his whip through the air, making it whistle like a strong wind. He bragged that one day he would be as good as his Uncle Joe. The old trapper could whisk the button off a coat or knock a cigar from someone's mouth with his fifty-four-foot whip.

Clarissa moved out by the gates to listen to the shouts of children and the yapping of dogs. Today she felt peace among the noises.

When the supper bell rang, she followed the rest of the children indoors. She stopped to watch Caleb Rose, who was as meek and as mild a boy as any mistress could want, painting Santa Claus in watercolours on the dining room wall. He was finishing the tip of one of Santa's black boots, about to touch down on a red brick chimney. Clarissa made her way to her seat, feeling a delightful shudder, even though she likened Santa Claus to fairies.

"Let us say our prayers," Miss Elizabeth called, watching to see that her charges closed their eyes. The children mouthed Christmas prayers for the coming of the Christ

Child, and then ate quickly. The younger children were eager to go to bed and settle down to sleep as fast as they could, so that Christmas morning would come more quickly.

The mistress clapped her hands and dismissed the children. "Off to bed with you now, you younger boys and girls. Do not make a squeak," she warned. "You are in bed to sleep and to grow up while you are doing it."

"I'll shove off to bed, I will, too, Miss," Peter piped up, a mischievous look in his eyes, "if you'll answer a riddle."

"A riddle! Very well, seeing it is Christmas," Miss Elizabeth answered tolerantly. "A scrap of lenience for levity, if you will be brief."

Peter grinned and recited: "Four legs up cold as stone / Two legs down, flesh and bone / The head of the living in the mouth of the dead / Tell me the riddle and I'll go to bed."

Everyone laughed, and one of the orphans shouted, "I know – I know the answer!"

Peter said, "Whist!" with his finger to the side of his mouth, a habit of Housemother Simmons's. But Ben, a young boy who had a tight little face, a harelip and dark, sad eyes under blond hair, called out, "A man walking with a bark pot on his head, Miss."

Peter looked sullen. "'Tis the mistress I wanted to answer."

The mistress's eyebrows lifted. "Come on with it, then. What is the real answer? A bark pot? What is that?"

Peter crinkled his nose and replied, "Young Ben gave the

answer. A bark pot has four legs and is used to soak fishermen's sails and nets in tree bark and buds to keep them. And you thinks we're the ignorant ones. We knows what we knows, and you knows what you knows. I think meself, Miss, that makes us equal."

The mistress looked at him as if she wanted to set his eyes afloat in soapy water. Instead, she said in a tight voice, "Off with you now."

The young orphans were shooed up to bed. House helpers trailed behind, making sure the children went straight to their own dormitories. They ran off shouting riddles to each other. "What grows with its roots up?" called Ben.

The other orphans chanted, "Conkerbell! Conkerbell! Jack Frost hangs it from the roof. When it hits the ground, it rings."

Clarissa stopped to look at Caleb's painting of Santa. She had never seen a smiling Santa before; this one had a gold tooth, like the one Missus Frances had but rarely showed. Clarissa smiled back at Santa. Then she trailed the other girls, who were just starting up the stairs. Missus Frances called out, "Come into the parlour, girls." They all turned toward her, eager to get inside the staff's living quarters.

Clarissa had gotten only as far as the lounge. Now the girls followed Missus Frances through the lounge to a cozy little room. Clarissa once heard the older girls talking about the time Dr. Grenfell had asked them into the room. He sat in a big, green armchair, having a cup of tea from a small teapot that Missus Frances had placed on a little gateleg table covered in a white lace cloth. He had leaned forward with his cup, and told the girls about his grave ordeal on the ocean. He said he would never forget what happened after he set out with his dog team across a frozen bay to visit a patient. The wind changed, setting him adrift on a small pan of ice with his dogs; he had to sacrifice three of them to save himself and the other dogs. Clarissa's stomach turned over at the thought that, if Dr. Grenfell had died, she would not have had a doctor to help her walk – even with the help of crutches.

"Your mind, Clarissa, where has it taken off to now?" the mistress asked.

"It's right here inside my head," she answered and sat down quickly.

When the girls were seated, the mistress began to read the younger orphans' letters to Santa. Clarissa listened to their dreams: a new pair of boots, a doll, a windup truck, a cat . . . their own mothers and fathers.

"We can try to make your dreams come true, except for wishes to have parents and live animals," the mistress told them. She added, with a twist to her lips, "A cat would not last too long around here with all the dogs." She took pencils from a metal cup on the mantel and pulled sheets of paper from the tablet she held in her hands, passing one to each girl. "Here, write your wishes."

Clarissa looked at her and said softly, "My wish is to go home – and I'll go someday." Her words tightened over the promise to herself, her body trembling with anticipation.

The mistress lifted her eyebrows. "You seem contented here."

"That's because my mind doesn't put everything I think on my tongue," Clarissa answered.

"I dare say 'tis many a sigh you'll make before that day," Celetta said with a satisfied look on her face.

"I will go home," Clarissa answered in a stubborn voice, "and I will get well and have two good legs and strong arms and no more pain in my limbs." She lowered her head, and bit her lip to keep the tears inside.

Imogene rolled her eyes. The other girls pretended not to have heard as they wrote their wishes in front of the hearth, where fire leaped and danced above wood crackling in the large grate. A flanker popped out on the stone shelf and Cora exclaimed, "Strangers are coming!"

"A superstition, my dear," chided the mistress, "but someone *is* coming, and he is no stranger to the minds of children. It is time to take your letters, and toss them into the fireplace." Missus Frances's smile widened enough to show her gold tooth. She lifted her arms into the air. "Now!"

As quick as a wink, the children tossed their letters into the fire. "Close your eyes," the mistress added. "Now imagine the wings of the fire sending all the wishes up through the chimney out into the night. They shall fly on the wind through the sky and into Santa's castle at the North Pole."

"Well, I don't know, I'm sure," said Imogene. She had flung her letter with an uppity tilt to her nose, and kept her eyes open long enough to see the letters burn to ashes in the grate. "'Tis a little late to be choosing presents with Santa already in the skies. Sure, if he's on his way, he's on his way with whatever is already in his sleigh."

"That's the magic of it," Missus Frances said quickly, rising from her chair. "Off with you now; the dining room needs decorating. No beds for you, yet!"

The older orphan boys were coming from a gymnastic round in the playroom as the girls were leaving the mistresses' quarters. "What is it you're about in there?" asked Jakot, his lip turned up to his nose. The girls pretended they hadn't heard him. They went inside the dining room to decorate the boughs Jakot and other boys had left there, already bent with wire into wreaths. The pleasure of helping make Christmas happen surged through Clarissa as she helped trim the wreaths with bows of red ribbons. The girls put red tissue handkerchiefs on each bough of the Christmas tree, tucking them around green candles.

Clarissa and Cora were shaping stars from lead foil saved from pounds of tea and kept in an old tea chest, when they caught each other's eye. Clarissa knew Cora was thinking the same thing she was: that the box on Tea House Hill would be buried in snow sweeping in through the loose boards of the Tea House. It would be buried too deep for anyone to find and open. Clarissa crossed her fingers and made a wish: *Let the box be there next summer for us to open.*

After the girls finished decorating the dining room, Miss

Elizabeth called them upstairs. "Now, girls, it is time to make the candy bags for that special Christmas treat. Ilish is cutting out squares of gauze. She will help you."

The girls followed the mistress to the sewing room on the second floor. Ilish's round face was flushed with excitement as she passed the girls blocks of gauze, needles, and thread. They busied themselves sewing bags for the candy they and the younger children would receive. Imogene and Cora were getting on better than usual, tittering as if tickled by their own cute remarks. Clarissa was trying not to worry about Treffie in bed with a cold caught up on her chest. She was glad Treffie didn't have to go to the hospital. Her heart begged, *Please God, don't let Treffie be too sick to see the wreaths tied with red bows on the windows.*

It was just as well that Cora and Suzy were enjoying this Christmas. They both had a rattle on their chests. Cora didn't spend much time with her little sister because the two were in different dormitories; Suzy had made friends among the younger children. Clarissa glanced at Cora's happy face. She hoped it was influenza that Cora and her sister had, not consumption. Sometimes their colds cleared and they seemed almost healthy. Once the sisters got consumption, it would likely get rid of them, instead of them getting rid of it. Clarissa tried not to think about it as the girls finished stitching the bags. They piled them together before they left the room.

"Look, there's a star in front of the moon, the sign of civil weather for Santa's reindeer," Celetta called to the other girls as they entered the dormitory. The girls rushed to the window, getting there just as Housemother Simmons tapped on the door, calling to them to wash up and get to bed.

Clarissa lay in bed with the blankets pulled up to her chin, seeing the moon as a silver ornament hung in the sky. Christmas Eve was like a breath held in all over the world. She imagined reindeer, foxes, and bears in the woods dropping to their knees at the stroke of midnight in honour of Jesus's birthday. Maybe even husky dogs would kneel in their kennels. The wonder of Christmas made Clarissa's fingers and toes tingle. Her gaze stayed on the window. Anytime now, she might see the hooves of Santa's reindeer. *There's no point in having an imagination if you can't use it*, she thought. A cloud – or maybe Santa and his sleigh – crossed the moon, and darkness covered the window, filling the room and settling against her face like dark velvet. She fell asleep thinking of Christmas Day as a gift-wrapped box, its string ready to be burst and Christmas unwrapped.

It seemed that she had just fallen asleep when she woke up to a rustle in the dormitory. Her eyelashes lifted enough for her to see what had awakened her. Miss Elizabeth stood in the doorway holding a lamp while Missus Frances tiptoed to each bed, laying a Christmas stocking on the foot of it. Clarissa didn't wonder why Missus Frances was in the room and not Santa. Santa was only as real as her imagination; she closed her eyes and pretended it was Santa who was leaving the stockings.

Clarissa drifted back to sleep and dreamed that Santa had brought her a stocking full of reindeer turds. She stirred to the clanging of the bell as the dark drifts of night disappeared. There was a sudden clatter of voices in the hall. Some children were already on their way downstairs.

Clarissa sat on her bed and lifted her Christmas stocking. Inside were an orange, an apple, and some peanuts. She pulled out the orange wrapped in a tissue handkerchief and bit into it to pull off the rind; orange zest sprayed the cold air. Its scent mingled with the cool sweet scent of the apple. She knew the apple would have the star of Bethlehem in its centre. She would eat the apple and peanuts later.

Becky came into the bath and toilet room while Clarissa was brushing her teeth. "I saw Missus Frances put the Christmas stockings on our beds," she said, sounding disappointed.

Clarissa shrugged. "You can't expect Santa to fill stockings and do everything else. Besides, where would *he* get apples and oranges – and peanuts? He can't grow fruit and peanuts at the North Pole. You'll get a Christmas box downstairs."

Becky's freckled face relaxed and she went off to catch up with Imogene and the other girls, who had already left to go downstairs. Clarissa was left alone to take her time. She could hear the strains of the children's favourite carol, "Away in a Manger," from the Victrola as she made her way slowly down the steps. Someone was playing an accordion, too, but the sound was nothing more than a cough and a wheeze.

184

Most of the older children were in the hall when Clarissa got there. She accepted her slice of buttered bread for breakfast and waited for the dining room doors to open.

There were gasps as one child after another rushed into the dining room. They stopped to stare at a tree dressed in red bows, green candles, and silver stars. Gauze bags of hard candy were piled against its base. There was not a present in sight – just an empty wooden cot on rockers beside the tree.

"No presents! 'Tis just like when the world was in war, and four of the harbour's fellows went off to fight," Peter exclaimed.

"That's okay," Cora said. "'Tis fewer bad people in the world now because the good people killed them. Sure, that's a Christmas gift."

Imogene spoke up, lifting her tight, little chin to gain attention. "There could be lots of reasons why Santa didn't come. His suit could have caught on fire last year when he came down the chimney, and he was left with nothing to wear. Maybe there were too many children in the poor countries who needed regarding, or –" Her voice dropped to a whisper. "Santa could have just up and died."

The younger children looked at her with horrified faces before turning back to the tree. They were still staring at it when Miss Elizabeth swept into the room, in a navy dress with a square collar as white as new snow. The children didn't seem to notice she was holding a white bundle, until she announced, "We are celebrating the good tide of Christmas, knowing we are a privileged lot. Many children in the harbour didn't get their stockings filled. Most of them are thankful just to have stockings to put their feet in and a crust of bread and jam on their plates."

Clarissa thought of Esther. The image of the harbour girl, likely not much older than herself, drably dressed and grimy, was like a match put to a piece of coloured paper, burning to ashes what was left of her joyous emotions.

"Don't forget to thank God for Dr. Grenfell and the people around the world who help him keep you healthy and happy," the mistress said, her smile so wide that a dimple showed in one cheek. *It's not a dimple that God's fingertip pressed into her cheek*, Clarissa thought. *A dent is what it is, made by a smile her face wasn't ready for.*

"Yes, Miss Elizabeth." The children's voices rose in chorus, their heads bowed. "We thank God for the food we eat, and for the boots upon our feet. Father, we thank Thee."

The children's eyes widened as the mistress walked to the tree. She bent down to the wooden cot and laid the white bundle in it. "If the baby Jesus had not come, we would not have Christmas," she said gently. "This baby is a reminder that you are fortunate to have a home, and people in it who have become your family."

The children rushed to look at the pouty-faced baby, but Housemother Priddle, who took care of the younger children, shooed them away. "We don't want this motherless little child to catch the diseases that's around and about," she said with a firm lip. "He's under the tree to honour the baby Jesus."

The dining room door opened again, and an energetic young Ben galloped around the room on a hobby horse. Everyone was looking at the boy. They didn't see Santa Claus sneak in and stand right beside Treffie, who wouldn't be kept in bed on Christmas Day. When Treffie saw the black boots beside her, she looked up, wide-eyed, and let out a squeal. Her eyes closed and her body made a little shudder as she slid to the floor in front of the man in a Santa rig-out.

"Ho, Ho, Ho!" boomed a big voice Clarissa recognized as belonging to Dr. Curtis, an American who worked at the Grenfell Hospital. The big man scooped Treffie up in his arms and hurried to the tree with her. Her eyelashes flickered open and her eyes lit up as Santa put her down and grabbed up a bunch of candy bags. He passed a bag to Treffie. She looked up at him, her voice shaking. "I just took a little spell, Sir." Clutching her candy, she walked over and sat down beside Clarissa while Santa passed out the rest of the bags to the other children.

After the children sang "It came upon a Midnight Clear" with Missus Frances accompanying them on the piano, most of them scampered out into the hall. Clarissa and Cora stayed in the dining room. When Housemother Priddle went across the room to close a window, they hurried to get a close look at the baby.

Clarissa longed to lift the infant into her arms, to hold a beautiful, living doll for the first time. She knew that even if the housemother allowed her to pick him up, she wouldn't be able to hold him. He would slip from her arms, drop to the floor and get broken – maybe crippled. Then he would never get out of the orphanage.

Cora looked at the baby, her voice wistful. "I can't hold him because of my cough."

"And I can't hold him because of my infirmity," Clarissa said matter-of-factly.

Their chatter was stopped by the squawk of a tongue against their ears. "Out! Out! You young ones are not to be in here. Where is that wretched maid – housemother – whoever?" It was Miss Elizabeth in a fury, her arms beating the air as if the girls were flies she was trying to banish.

"We just wanted to look at the baby," Clarissa tried to explain, knowing the woman's Christmas spirit must be on its way out already.

"Can we see the baby shortened?" Cora asked. "I've never seen a baby shortened."

"No, the child is a New Year's gift for some family. They'll have the joy of shortening him at three months. And the means to do it."

Clarissa imagined the party there would be on the day of the shortening. The baby, bundled up like a papoose since he was born, would finally get his legs loose. Dressed in booties, a knitted sweater, drawers and a cap, he would kick with all his might and blow bubbles in the face of anyone who pecked his cheek and cooed, "Coochy-coo."

I must have been shortened myself when I was a baby,

Clarissa thought. *Maybe just in time to get a few kicks in before the ailment got at me.*

"Next you will want to lift him!" Miss Elizabeth shuddered. "You know what can come from being dropped."

"No, we don't," Cora whispered into Clarissa's ear as they hurried into the hall, where children were squealing and laughing. Ben had found a present in his locker. A bright spin top was twirling on the floor. The other children ran to their lockers and lifted the covers; inside were gifts wrapped in green or red tissue paper. There were pocket combs, barrettes, knitted stockings, wooden spin tops, boats, harmonicas, a checkerboard, books – some with pictures. There were dolls made from bottles and dressed by Miss Pritcher, the seamstress. Boys who got push cars and tractors were soon truckling them across the hardwood floor.

Clarissa took what felt like a book from her locker, and was tearing the red tissue off when she saw, out of the corner of her eye, Missus Frances looking at her. The mistress crooked her finger and Clarissa laid down her gift and went toward the office, wondering what trouble she had gotten herself in now. Missus Frances closed the door and sat down. Clarissa stayed standing.

"You have another Christmas box, Clarissa, a white muff from your mother," the mistress informed her. Clarissa's heart leaped. Her family hadn't forgotten her!

The mistress shook her head. "It is quite impractical for you to wear a muff with your disability, even if there was no weakness in your left arm. We will keep it in the office. Besides, the other children will feel left out if they know you received an extra Christmas box. You cannot be selfish, Clarissa."

Clarissa stared at the mistress, wanting to beg for her muff, cry for it, knock the mistress to the floor with her crutches and search the big, wooden drawers in the office, but she knew there was nothing she could say or do to get her muff. Once the mistress set her mind, there was no changing it.

Clarissa lumbered out of the mistress's office, not caring how much noise she made as she went to get her book. Cora and Treffie came up beside her and sat down on the locker. Treffie's pale face was anxious. "I wanted a sister for my dolly," she whispered. She looked down at the book on her knee. "A book is no good to me."

"Now, don't be putting on a long face," Cora told her. "Santa knew what you needed to bring out yer readin' voice."

"It's true, Treffie," said Clarissa. "Reading is a lot of fun. It will knock the loneliness out of your head for hours at a time. You'll love *Heidi*."

"I don't know how to read," Treffie said, her eyes downcast. "I don't remember ever pitching me eyes on books before I cum here. Sure, I don't know what the black marks mean."

"You'll learn here, then," Cora promised. "Fast, too, when yer feeling better and Miss Ellis gets ahold of you."

Treffie's eyes brightened. "I'll be glad then."

Clarissa sulked all the way through the salmon and rice dinner. She tried to listen to her sister-self talking. *You can't be getting two gifts when everyone else gets one. You like the book you got. It's yours; you don't have to take it back to the library. It's just as well you can't have the muff. If you wore it on the sled, Peter and Jakot might grab it and that would be the last you'd see of your mother's gift.*

After dinner, Clarissa went into the study and sat at the table, leafing through an issue of *Among The Deep Sea Fishers*, a magazine founded by Dr. Grenfell to tell the world about the people of his mission. The "Children's Page" had a story about the need for a Home. Clarissa looked at the sketch of the brick orphanage. Little girls, in wide-brimmed hats, flowered dresses, and striped and plain knitted stockings, were walking up the concrete steps beneath the entrance's arch. Clarissa imagined The Home being just as perfect in real life. It likely could be, if everyone followed the motto: "A long pull, a strong pull, and a pull together."

She searched until she found the Christmas issue from 1915. She read, as she had last year, about her first Christmas away from home. She was at the Grenfell Hospital. On Christmas Day, every patient well enough was moved to the same ward. There were shrieks of delight when Santa Claus stood in the doorway with a bag slung over his shoulder. Clarissa's eyes brightened as she read about herself: ". . . Clarissa Dicks found somebody's lap to bury her head in and tried valiantly to surpass George in screaming. It was impossible for Santa Claus to make any advance, whatever gift he offered the two, and not until he had removed his mask would Clarissa deign to peek through her fingers and give him a shy smile as she accepted a big darling doll."

Clarissa smiled at this image of herself. She closed the magazine and pushed herself to her feet. She lifted her chin. *I'm not a baby and I am not going to cry*. She'd take a lesson from Johnny, a little boy from Labrador. Once, after some older boy had picked on him, Clarissa had gone to comfort him. He had shrugged, and said with a grin, "Whenever I feel like crying, I smile instead. That's what everyone wants to see: a bright face like a bright day."

She would lie in bed, snug under her blankets and counterpane and read her Christmas book. *Little Women* was sure to make her smile.

Disparity

Children holding arms full of toys chime,
"Give me . . . Give me . . . GIVE ME . . ."
Children in other lands holding out their
empty hands.

The Man Who Liked Christmas As Much As A Turkey

In my childhood days of Christmas Eves past, amid the constant static coming over the airwaves, I often pressed my ear against the radio on the shelf beside our kitchen table and listened to *A Christmas Carol*. Not knowing what Marley's spirit and the ghosts of Christmases past, present, and future looked like was as mysterious for me as the voices.

When the spirits spoke, I felt drawn into a tunnel of black fog. I imagined a ghost in eerie garments swirling around Scrooge, its hollow sounds mingling with the Atlantic Ocean's howling winds sweeping in over the cold waters of Hibb's Cove and blowing through the crevices of the cliffs.

Slivers of conversation stayed with me: ". . . darkness is cheap and Scrooge liked it. Tiny Tim's limbs were supported by an iron frame and a crutch. . . . Tiny Tim wanting to hear the pudding singing in the cupper. Tiny Tim did not die."

When he was a child, Ebenezer had been left alone in a boarding school at Christmas while his peers went home with their families, some to hold a newborn sibling and to feel the warmth and smell the sweetness of the child. Maybe no one had ever hugged him nor told him he was loved. Ebenezer's childhood self had been stunted by neglect; that child was still inside him, but lost. A season that brings out the child in humans, to expect gifts from the heart and from the hand, could not stir the adult heart of a man who had not been given Christmas as a child. It was kept from him and he had become embittered and unwilling to give Christmas to anyone or keep it for himself. Just as he was shunned as a boy, now he shunned other people. Just as circumstances had separated him as a child from his family, now he, himself, through insecurity, separated himself from family and acquaintances. He found it easier to get love out of money than to give money out of love for his human fellows.

A psychiatrist could have easily analyzed Scrooge's childhood and how it affected his adult behaviour. The first ghost took Ebenezer back to the boarding school. He wept at the sight of his forgotten self reading alone by a feeble fire while the other children were gone home for the holidays. His friends were in books: Ali Baba, the Genie, Robinson Crusoe, and others. Ebenezer's father would not allow him to leave the boarding house until Fan, his little sister, prevailed to have her brother home for the holidays. By this time, his spirit, which had never been nurtured into becoming a generous one, had shrivelled, and his sense that no one would make a place for him in the world had been entrenched. It was up to him to make his own security. As an adult he did not spend his money. He kept it for comfort and security.

Fan died after marrying and having Fred, her only child. Belle, the young woman who had offered Ebenezer her love, had not been able to entice him into nurturing that love. He had chosen rather to love what she called his golden idol. When two gentlemen showed up at Scrooge's place of work asking help for the poor, they remarked, "They [the poor] choose Christmas to ask for help because it is a time of all others, when want is keen and abundance rejoices."

Scrooge's abundance did not rejoice. It was nipped in a tight fist. The old merchant was satisfied that he helped the establishments of the Union Workhouses or the Treadmill and the Poor Law, which provided for public relief and assistance for the poor. According to the gentlemen, many could not get into those places and others would rather die than go to such wretched establishments.

"If they would rather die," said Scrooge in his grating voice, "they had better do it and decrease the surplus population."

Scrooge had money because he worked for it. It was the security blanket he wrapped around himself day and night, trying in vain to get warm. The cold spirit within him froze his old features, nipped his pointed nose, shrivelled his cheeks, made his eyes red, his thin lips blue, and stiffened his gait.

There was no one to accept the challenge to try and change the man who knew he had no value to anyone outside his money. Gossip employed the tongues of people who got great pleasure from taking the name of Scrooge on their tongues as if it were a sour pickle.

"Thank God I'm not like Scrooge," people exclaimed, all the while wishing they could be enough like him to have his money bag. Some would have probably changed places with him, taking his meanness and all to get what they wanted most in life – riches. It was envy that stirred the tongues of these people; in their hearts, they were as mean as he.

When Charles Dickens wrote *A Christmas Carol* in 1843, he painted a picture, not only of Scrooge, but also of the people surrounding him. Rich and poor were miserly in what they could afford to give and didn't – a generous spirit.

"What reason have you to be happy?" asked Scrooge of his nephew. "You're poor enough."

"What reason have you to be morose? You're rich enough," the nephew returned gaily.

After Scrooge's enlightening visits from the spirits, after their Christmas Eve's visitations on a world past, present, and future, he seemed to have mined his flesh-and-blood heart from his gold one. He met one of the portly gentlemen who had earlier solicited funds for the poor. When he whispered in the man's ear promises of money, including back payments, the fellow almost lost his breath.

It was said at first that "Scrooge didn't keep Christmas. He left it alone." In the end it was said that "Scrooge knew how to keep Christmas well."

Hopefully Scrooge knew how to keep all seasons well by giving the spirit of Christmas all year, so that the neglected Tiny Tims of his community did not remain children of want. They would be joyous in exclaiming, "God bless us every-one!"

Christmas Giving

Americans kick off Christmas with Thanksgiving celebrations. They set off on their Christmas shopping spree with platitudes like "It's not the things we have, but the things we give that make us rich" jingle-belling through their heads.

Unfortunately for Canadians, Thanksgiving is so far behind us we've forgotten what we learned from it. Perhaps the only way some of us will get through Christmas shopping is if we go back to Thanksgiving and draw from its spirit, one that teaches us to be thankful for life as it has favoured us: with little or much.

It is easy for us to be so preoccupied with "buying Christmas" that we forget its meaning. Some of us become depressed as we move through stores with expectations that exceed our means. We don't want to live according to our needs but according to whatever means we can. Many of us have not learned that the wise use of one talent can bring as much value to our lives and the lives of others as five talents.

People like the late Dave Butler have one special talent:

the gift of humour. Dave, who was crippled with arthritis and blind from diabetes, died just before Christmas 2005, but not before one last laugh. Despite his pain he always wanted to be around people, helping where he could.

When his church group was packing Christmas boxes, Dave offered to help.

"You can lick the stickers indicating if the box is for a boy or girl," a Christmas organizer suggested.

This once healthy, handsome man, now bowed by disease, lifted his head to one side and smiled. "I can't do that," he said. "I don't have a licker licence."

He would have enjoyed the words on a calendar created by artists who paint with their mouths and feet: "The heart that finds joy in small things. . . in all things each day is a wonderful gift."

Helen Keller lived inside a body that was a dark and lonely place. It let in no sound or light. While she may not have had all her senses, those she had compensated for those she didn't have. She had enough common sense to realize that the best gifts we have to give are those within ourselves.

In an essay published in *The Atlantic Monthly*, Helen said, ". . . only the deaf appreciate hearing and only the blind appreciate sight."

Keller wrote about things she would like to see and hear if she was given the gift of sight and sound for only three days. They were common things that we take for granted every day. Helen saw Christmas best from inside her heart: A star shining in stillness and purity in a dark sky, above a nativity scene holding a new family in the midst of bleating animals.

We too can see the things that matter from our hearts, if we do not allow human nature to get in the way of a Divine event. So many of us rush around stores hardly knowing what we are doing. We find ourselves in a darker world than the one Keller escaped. Perhaps it is time to step out of the long lineups and stand apart. Listen! Hark! The herald angels sing. It never fails to lift my spirit. I love the sounds of those familiar carols piped into stores, and the feelings generated by them: the gaiety, the triumph, and the overwhelming sense of being a part of something great and miraculous. Peace on earth becomes peace internally.

Gift-giving means something only when it originates from a heart that longs to give. We can see it as an opportunity to participate, in a tangible way, in expressing our appreciation for those who touch our lives. A card of appreciation can be a gift to someone who doesn't realize how much she means to others.

It takes a season like Christmas to force a kind of generosity missing in most of us the rest of the year. Still, we could do less shopping for gifts, and give more of what we already have to give – ourselves. A gift that lasts comes from the bottom of the heart, not from the bottom of a purse or the swipe of a credit card. We can celebrate each day as a gift of opportunity to invoke the spirit of generosity: To see a need and respond to it without the wrappings of a Christmas season. I remember hugging an elderly relative, whose faded blue eyes looked into mine as he exclaimed, "It's *some* long since I had a hug."

Maybe it's a while since a senior had homemade bread, baked beans, or some other favourite dish. Some of us can fulfill such longings. For a senior citizen who can't get out, a takeout dinner might be a gastric delight. A lonely person who has no children at home can reach out, and borrow someone else's children. That person can invite the children's parents to tag along, and put up their feet while someone else cooks the weary parents a holiday treat.

"Christmas won't be like Christmas without any presents," grumbled Jo, in the opening line of Louisa M. Alcott's *Little Women*.

Fortunately, Jo and her sisters did not have Christmas without having presents. They each received a copy of *Pilgrim's Progress*. It wasn't much by today's standards, but the book helped to serve the purpose Marmee had in mind for her four daughters.

More than a hundred years later, we search for gifts to give our children, hoping to satisfy the materialistic wants bound up in their hearts. We hope these will be perfect gifts, ones that will hold those special memories that will glow through the density of years to come. Some of us think we can do this by buying the biggest and most expensive gifts.

In *Little Women* it was said about Marmee, "There never

was such a woman for givin' away vittles and drinks, clothes and firin's." Marmee knew enough not to borrow from the future to pay for the day's happiness. Her daughters learned that giving up something for Christmas is as important a part of Christmas as giving and receiving. Despite their own plans for a good breakfast, Marmee's "little women" took their cream and muffins to the mother of a new baby and five other children huddled in one bed.

The girls learned that no one owed them Christmas. They had done nothing to deserve the miraculous thread of happiness that joins the hearts of strangers to friends and family at Christmastime. But that morning, as "little women" brightened the lives of another family, they found that Christmas giving is Christmas lived to its fullest: tangible evidence of the trinity of faith, hope, and charity.

Children Of Christmas

As you rush through shopping malls gathering up Christmas gifts for those you love, you may be too busy to notice a lone figure. But someday, if you stop and observe all the characters on the Christmas stage, you'll be sure to see her.

She's the little girl moving up the aisle, eager to have her picture taken with Santa Claus, her big eyes reflecting the sparkling clarity of the season as she hastens toward her dream. Soon one of the old gent's helpers speaks to her. Long lashes fall against soft flushed cheeks as she draws back – a tiny, forlorn creature twisting a half-hanging button on her shabby coat. She doesn't have the money to pay for her Christmas dream, and among the hurrying Christmas shoppers there is no one who will take the time to give a gift to one small child. The stars in the child's eyes are suddenly muddled with tears.

This child is one of the children of Christmas: those in need, those who stand alone.

The child of Christmas is the elderly lady sitting in an old folks' home searching for familiar faces as her rocking chair makes the same monotonous creak day after day. She's the widowed mother who waits in a big, empty house, her loneliness made almost unbearable by the absence of her grown children. She is the person who has been handed the verdict: cancer. And the sentence: a year or two.

The child of Christmas is the boy who has had his world torn apart as the parents he loves go separate ways. He is the teenager who gets showered with gifts when what he hungers for is family closeness.

The child of Christmas is the single man who has no one to share his Christmas dinner. He's the elderly man who opens unwanted gifts. What he really wants is a visit from his family. He's the man who has only a pillow to hug.

The child of Christmas is someone who has no faith in himself and no hope in his world. He is someone who has never learned how to accept love or give it. He is all the people who have not found a place in anyone's heart.

Those who focus on the superficial aspects of Christmas rather than on the first child of Christmas may never notice those children of God. Each of them requires gifts that are already stored within us to give: a touch, a smile, hospitality, a word of praise, an ear that listens. Tangible expressions should also be given with an open heart, for the meaning of Christmas comes through the giving by those who have to those who have not.

Each of us may have only one candle, but with it we can

light a thousand candles in dark corners, for it is in the darkness of life that our lights can shine their brightest, and make Christmas a giant candle drawing the children of Christmas away from the aloneness of their lives.

A Child Of Want

Laughter, light and bubbly, rose and fell as the subway train raced on its course, its white eye picking its way through subterranean blackness, hurrying its passengers toward another Christmas Day. Friends chatted, strangers accepted smiles from strangers: all intoxicated with the season's magical suspense, each eagerly awaiting surprises.

All except for the young mother holding, in the curve of her drooping arm, a squirming, wailing child. Despair, like a dark shroud, seemed to merge her with the night outside, and yet it silhouetted her against the atmosphere of lightened hearts. Just then, the train creaked to a halt.

A teenager grabbed a seat vacated by a scurrying passenger. Her blue eyes, lit like Christmas bulbs, looked toward the mother whose arm was dragged down by her child. The girl seemed to look down at her own empty hands, and then back to the mother. A question tumbled from her lips. "Please, may I hold your baby?"

The mother drew back as if the question had scorched her

senses. Her eyes looked out as if from punctured black holes in a tired, white face. Christmas seemed months – years – away from her. Her child, his dirty face pinched in pain or hunger, lay against her arm like last year's unopened Christmas gift.

The teenager reached gently to unburden the mother's tired arm, exclaiming all the while about the baby's dimples and soft hazel eyes. Slowly, moment by moment, she unwrapped the child before the mother's listless eyes. A reluctant smile crept across her face, obliterating harsh tracks made, perhaps, by her rough journey through motherhood.

The girl pulled a fruit juice box from her coat pocket and looked hesitantly toward the mother, who nodded her assent. The child sucked the juice box dry and settled into sleep. Then the girl seemed to hesitate, but only for a moment. One hand reached into the pocket of her jeans and pulled out a twenty-dollar bill. Without looking at the mother, she thrust it into the pocket of the baby's thin, torn suit. It seemed then that the mother's shoulders lifted.

After the girl passed the sleeping baby back to his mother, and got off at the next station, the mother's eyes met the darkness outside the train as if seeing a star of hope lighting the way for her and her baby through the dark journey of the Christmas season.

The rest of us were left silent – as if thinking of all the babies who have not, through the centuries, lain in the proverbial warm manger in swaddling clothes, babies who have not had rich kings from the East bearing gifts or a father as supportive as Joseph. For the first time, some of the passengers may have learned that the children of ignorance, peering from the skirts of Scrooge's Christmas ghost, with pinched, unhappy faces, could be us, concerned only with our own superficial preparations, while a teenager became a nova to a child of want.

The Poetics
Of Christmas

The dance of poetry punctuates every Christmas.

The Colours Of Christmas

Thinking of Christmas gifts, and plans,
I made my headlong rush through shopping malls.
Stopped by an object in the way of my foot,
I heard a woman's voice
taking me past carol singing, tinsel and candy canes
to a white cane held by a little boy.
I followed the tip to the little hand holding it, and up to a little face.
The boy's closed lids didn't stir to the voice of a woman chiding him:
"Watch where you're going."

It was I who should have watched where I was going –
stopped to see a little boy who had no light beneath his shadowed domes:
a child who seemed to be sleepwalking through
the colours of Christmas.

"You have to get used to it,"
the caregiver continued.
And then I saw the child's eyes open
as if he was caught in the colour of night,
straining to see
the colours of Christmas.

I went on my way, wishing him sight.

Until then, I want him to have
the gift of holding all the good times in his life,
in memories that come in colour.

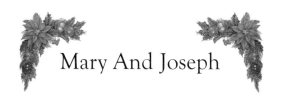

Mary And Joseph

Mary's slim hands trembled,
the rhythmic thump of her heart
thrashed out her thought:
How can this be?
Her voice came in a whisper:
"I know no man."
"The Holy Ghost," the angel answered,
"shall come to you and you
shall bear the Son of God."

Then,
even as she clutched at words
to thrust the angel's prophecy away,
faith sprang a seed within her heart,
and words that stood
still trembling on her lips:
"I know no man,"
were silenced by this truth:
God is the author of impossibilities.

Meekly, her faith released submission.
Surrender became sweet.

Her thoughts went swiftly to her man.
She ran to tell him all.

No joyous light lit Joseph's eyes.
Startled, he looked at her.
The slender girl stood unafraid,
her big, dark eyes in lucent innocence.
His doubt made him abrupt:
"What are you saying, Woman;
what words are these?"
Cool fingers touched his hand.
"Joseph!" Her voice was sure.
"An angel came. He witnessed to my heart
that strange and wondrous things
would be of us a part.
It does not matter what the people think."

"I, too, must think," he said,
then quietly left her side.
The cry upon her lips, compelling him to stay,
fell dead.
God's love rose full inside her heart.
No other love could be as great.
Assurance filled her being

that Joseph's love would be sustained
by God's unbounded love.
Carpenter Joseph worked his trade,
his heart as knotted as the wood
cradled in his hands.
Pride in his own manhood
pushed doubt in front.
How could young Mary's love
demand so much of his?
Voices whispered through his mind:
Women say strange things to cover up
when having sinned.
Panic seized his heart.
He'd have to give her up.
He tossed that night,
then fell asleep.

Dreams forced a sweat out on his brow,
Mary stoned stoned stoned.
Its echoes beat inside his head
like heavy, falling stones.
His cries into the shadows
were groans of shame for lack of faith.
His doubt had stamped her an adulteress.

And then one dream laid all
the other dreams to rest.

An angel came with "Peace, be still"
to reach inside his thoughts
and throw out doubt.
Mary's destiny and his
were interwoven with a child who was
Jehovah's Son wrapped in humanity.
Messiah would be born
to free the human heart from sin:
This story through the ages
written with a diamond point,
engraved in sacrificial blood,
Divine Love, unharnessed,
poured out upon the human race.

Through the dark cloak of night,
joy broke through as radiant as the morning sun.

Surrender became sweet.

Mary

Whispers brushed along Mary's spine
like hissing snakes,
as she passed by people in the village.
Old women's eyes
marked out her belly.

Villagers waited for the evidence
that time would bring.
Their snickers came:
"Virgin? Adulteress!"

Caught in the sovereignty
of Divine Love,
Mary showed no shame.
Her steady look made people
thirst in anger for her stoning.
But Joseph, kind man,

had dreams that gave him strength
to take to wife a maid
whose body cradled a child.
Not his!

Dear God, then whose?
And God distinctly answered, "Mine!"

Christmas Wish

I wish this year
Christmas would mean
that while we hang up stockings
the naked feet of children
will not run cold,
but fill warm stockings.

I wish that every child
will have a belly full
of food that satisfies,
their little cheeks aglow
like ruby ornaments,
their eyes alight like Christmas bulbs.

I wish that little hands held up like cups
will hold their fill
of precious gifts
to stir their hearts to love and joy.

But wishes can't come true
unless we help them to:
when you and I will care enough
to fill where there is emptiness
and empty where there's terrible fullness
that in the darkness of the children's night
a Christmas star will shine.

Mary Wanting One Wise Woman

Melchior, Gaspar, Balthazar riding the night
before a star of wonder
. . . stand in a stable holding out gifts.

"Wise they are," says Joseph.
"Wise they'd be," says Mary,
"if they'd give us their robes to cut the chilly air.
"What are they doing
bringing gold, frankincense, and myrrh?
"The gold we can use in trade,
but what of frankincense and myrrh?
"To be frank, I'm not up to
chewing gum or burning incense,
though a fresh scent would come in handy
in this stable.
"I'm thirsty and hungry."
Says the shepherd boy, "I could milk a sheep."

"Baa," says the sheep.

"Shush," cautions Mary. "You'll wake little Jesus."

"I could wake the day," crows the rooster.

"Moo," says a cow. "I have *moolk*."

"I could lay an egg," clucks a hen squatting in the hay.

Says Joseph, "I'm so hungry I could eat a horse."

"Hee haw," brays the donkey. "Not me!"

"I'd like chicken soup, latkes, and a nice cup of tea,"
murmurs Mary. "Where's one wise woman when you need
her?"

The Christmas Mouse

'Twas the night before Christmas when all through the house
a creature was stirring: a little white mouse.
He was dressed all in red
from his heels to his head,
running the floor as fast as he could,
stopping to tip his Santa Claus hood.
He scampered upon a little boy's bed,
his furry white toes pointing ahead.
He sniffed at the boy's ruddy, cold nose,
then burrowed himself under the clothes.
There was neither a stir nor a squeal in the bed.
But out on the floor he heard a soft sound:
a stocking descending in a long, hard mound.
He got fast to the stocking, grabbed up his share,
and without Merry Christmas in the little boy's ear,
he went under the bed and munched on an apple.
It went crunch, and crack, and made a loud snapple.

The little boy woke in the dark of the night
to sounds of the mouse taking a bite.
He ran from the room with a scream that was loud;
his bedclothes all settling down like a cloud.
The mouse crept back on top of the bed,
"This is a good Christmas," he said.
He let out a burp and then not one peep.
With his belly plumb full he settled in sleep,
while all through the halls and the stairs of the house
the little boy's dad searched for a GREAT BIG MOUSE.

Christmas Is

Children's laughter ringing the bell of beginnings, pealing hope to elderly people whose clappers are cracked or gone, the elderly walking back in time by the light of children's eyes in unblemished faces, the remembrance of their own children, a comfort on dark nights.

Having a grandfather who minds when he was so little all he wanted for Christmas was a 'ammer, nain, and chine (hammer, nail and twine).

Remembering invisible threads of well-being joining strangers and friends on Christmas Eve, in good times and bad.
Infinite love sent from heaven to earth.

Santa Claus, skinny and pipe-free, so he can be a good role model.

Times when we were little and wished we were big.

Memory taking us on a journey back inside our souls – a journey that reaches back to childhood when our hands felt for packages bearing our name, a precious gift inside.
A time when we wrap our presence around the presents we give our children, knowing that when they tire of our presents they won't tire of our presence (until they are teenagers).

Singing Christmas carols in the spirit of harmony with all the peoples of the world.

Rachel's Children

Lullabies were hushed
and last kisses brushed
on tiny cheeks.
Amid the whispering breath of sleeping children,
men with evil eyes and pointing swords
came to find the Child.
Mothers,
hearing the rampage
of a thousand hooves,
trembled at the thundering
in their heads,
and ran to hold their babes
before the onslaught
of the flaming swords.
Little boys turned toward a glint,
then, smiling, reached to touch
the naked steel
as it touched them.

Lies that faltered on the mothers' lips:
"A daughter!"
were whipped away by soldiers' sneers.
The slayers stripped the bodies bare
and left them cold.

All through that starless night,
Rachel wept tears of blood,
while Mary's Child
wove sweet dreams.
But in through Mary's thoughts
a premonition stirred,
and filled the years
until at last
Rachel's cry and Mary's
became one.

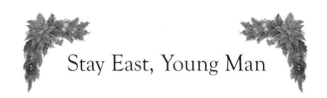 Stay East, Young Man

My son, with his bride, is unravelling the miles
from the west coast of this easterly island
to Canada's Fort Nelson,
riding a bus and thrumming his guitar.

Young men hoping for work here
stay
twanging guitars for sweet vibrations,
clang xylophones as if coins are dropping
on a sultry night in the hideaway.

A lazy breeze
lifts summer leaves against a window
while my mind drifts beyond sweet vibrations
to wonder how long my son will stay
away.
The Sliks,

faces bathed in flickering hues of purple and green
grunge the air until my ears are pulsing.
Will they stay to cast music on water
hoping to find bread?

Will Christmas come and my son's music
be in the air elsewhere?
Can I wish a boomerang for Christmas?
Will he follow it home
or will I be left with images of him
as a little boy under the Christmas tree
dangling icicles into his mouth
as if they were spaghetti?

An Empty Nest In
The Christmas Tree

There are times when we want it quiet:
no children shouting, spilling drinks, and whinging.
Then suddenly the house that used to stretch and call
sleeps.
We lie in bed afloat in shadowy dreams.
We stir, surface, listen,
open our eyes,
expecting the sweet breath of children on our faces,
arms flung around our necks to anchor us
to a new day and them,
but there is only a cat
to jump on the bed, sniff,
knead its paws.

The Christmas tree is silent,
no swinging of ornaments as children
dig their heads under branches to

233

bring out gifts.
The day holds in its breath
and is as silent as midnight in Christmas light.
And we wish, how we wish for
the rolling laughter of children,
and a Christmas past to gatecrash the present.

I follow a Christmas trail back through memories:
all that will hold me through this empty Christmas.
Like a squirrel I hoard them,
bring them back,
sit and look at the tree remembering when my nest
was warm with babies, memories of them flying away for
Christmas,
hopes of them coming back, filling the nest again with little
ones.

Sometimes they do.

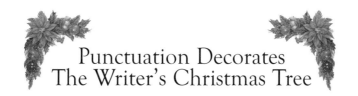

Punctuation Decorates
The Writer's Christmas Tree

Velvet green *dashes* rush in –
stretch out on tree needles, looking pretty.
Question marks arrive as couples dressed in silver,
face each other,
hang on boughs upside down,
fasten to silver *asterisks*.
Less than and *greater than* get together to make a
diamond ornament.
One *solidus* leans to touch another on the same branch.
She exclaims, "I'm *Virgule!*
"And you can kiss my *asterisk*."
A *backslash* tries to come on to *Virgule*;
he can't reach her.
Two *commas* pause on the tip of a branch
holding a toy Santa Claus between them.
They drop Mr. Claus and face each other,
coming together: a red heart.

Ellipses run around the tree dotting it in coloured lights,
chasing away *colons, semicolons,* and *periods.*
An *ampersand* sits quietly on a bough, legs crossed,
and nods to another *ampersand.*
He jumps down and sits under the tree,
reaches for a gift.
Dashes rush to be close;
question marks run across the wrappings;
quotation marks poise like fingers
ready to hold words whispering through tree tinsel,
"What is in the Christmas boxes?"
On the way out the door,
two *exclamation points* get the ball rolling for a New Year's
Eve party,
rushing and following *question marks* who keep asking the
time.
They already know where the party will be:
Grammar is away.

Christmas Journey

Accordion pockets are empty,
chocolate delights, once sitting pretty,
broken, sugary entrails drained . . .
round taut ornaments lie in square boxes,
mysterious gifts unwrapped to be
ordinary items found in stores all year.

We end this journey into an inflated season,
let it pass Old Christmas Day
and fizzle out
as a new year
comes in.

In the after-effects of trying
to buy a Christmas Spirit
that came free,

love remains.

Christmas Lore

If a Christmas visitor shows up during supper hour on Christmas Eve, he is given no hospitality. Instead, he is ridden home on a gully stick.

In times past, a Christmas back junk from white birch was laid across the fire on Christmas Eve to invoke good luck.

Those who sneak to the barn to watch animals kneel to pray on Christmas Eve will have their blood turned to water.

On Christmas Day, it was traditional to blow the pudding out of the pot. As the pudding was lifted, a gun – using blanks – was fired into the air.

It was a Christmas custom to load a gun with powder, to fire as one celebrated Christmas with a dram of rum and three cheers.

A Christmas box was once a collection box for gathering coins to give to the poor.

The Christmas cactus forewarns of death. If it doesn't bloom at Christmastime, death is coming.

In the 1800s, mummers often stole an item from one house where they were allowed in, and left it at another house.

NEWFOUNDLAND FAMILIES LOYAL TO ENGLAND BAKED A KING CAKE as a yearly tradition. Inside the cake was a charm. Whoever found it in their piece of cake was king for the day.

MUMMERS BROUGHT GOOD LUCK to a household if, when they came into a house, they counted the four corners of a room and made a wish.

SALTED, DRIED CODFISH was eaten on St. Stephen's Day as Christmas fish.

LUGGING WAS AN ANCIENT PORT DE GRAVE CUSTOM. If a man was caught working on St. Stephen's Day, he would be made to sit on a ladder. He was then tied to it. If he resisted, a group of men would lug him all over the place, giving him a bumpy ride.

TO HANG A NEW YEAR'S CALENDER before the new year is to invite bad luck.

THE BURNING OF THE CLAVIE was a ritual where blubber barrels were split and set alight, smoking the sky to open the new year.

IF A DARK-HAIRED STRANGER CROSSES THE THRESHOLD on New Year's Day, persons of that household will have a year of good luck.

IT WAS BAD LUCK to leave the tree up after Old Christmas Day.

TEAK DAY (OLD CHRISTMAS DAY), JANUARY 6, was once a day when children dressed up in old clothes, cut themselves a stick each, and went about cracking anyone they saw who was not wearing a piece of green ribbon.

PUBLISHING CREDITS AND REFERENCES

"The Christmas Story: Past and Present," *The R-B Weekender*, Dec. 24–30, 1983.

"Blue Slippers for Betty," *The Newfoundland Herald*, Dec. 19–25, 2004. CBC Christmas Reading 2003.

"Old Nart," *Widdershins*, Jesperson Publishing, 1996. *The Downhomer*, Dec. 1997. *The Compass*, Dec. 23, 1983, also performed as part of a Christmas program at Sir Wilfred Grenfell College.

"Widdershins," *Widdershins*, Jesperson Publishing, 1996. *The Downhomer*, Dec. 1997. *The Compass*, Dec. 23, 1983, also performed as part of a Christmas program at Sir Wilfred Grenfell College.

"Surviving Christmas in One Piece or More," *TV Topics*, Dec. 19, 1981.

"Christmas at the North Pole," *The R-B Weekender*, Dec. 22–28, 1984.

"Cabbage Patch Craze (The Cabbage Kids' Scratch Patch)." "Things to Talk About," *The Compass*, Dec. 14, 1983.

"Christmas Homecoming."A winner in CBC's Christmas Contest 1994. *Yuletide*, Christmas 2002. Robinson-Blackmore Ltd.

"Taking Christ Out of Christmas." "Things to Talk About," *The Compass*, Dec. 18, 1985.

"Christmas Giving," *The Compass*, Dec. 17, 1986.

"The Yuletide Card," *The Newfoundland Herald*, Dec. 24, 1988.

"Christmas Shopping." "Things to Talk About," *The Compass*, Dec. 2, 1987.

"Shopping for Christmas," *The Newfoundland Herald*, Dec. 22–28, 1990.

"Taking Shopping Out of Christmas." "Things to Talk About," *The Compass*, Dec. 12, 1984.

"Santa is a Mummer," *The Newfoundland Herald*, Dec. 21–27, 1991.

"Clausophobia." "Things to Talk About," *The Compass* Dec. 22, 1982.

"An Old-Fashioned Christmas." "Things to Talk About," *The Compass*, Dec. 23, 1986.

"A Family's Christmas Gift." "Things to Talk About," *The Compass*, Dec. 28, 1983.

"Christmas Wish," *The Compass*, Dec. 23, 1987.

"O Christmas Tree." "Things to Talk About," *The Compass*, Dec. 28, 1987.

"Children of Christmas." "Things to Talk About," *The Compass*, Dec. 23, 1987. *The Humber Log*, Dec. 1997.

"A Child of Want," *A Nearly Perfect Christmas*, CBC Contest Anthology 2001.

"Unlikely Mothers," *Good Tidings*, Dec. 1999.

"The Christmas Caller." "Things to Talk About," *The Compass*, Dec. 1983.

"Mummering's the Word," *Globe & Mail*, Dec. 27, 1985.

"Mary and Joseph," *Good Tidings*, Nov.–Dec. 1975.

"The Gift of Love." "Things to Talk About," *The Compass*, Dec. 3, 1985.

"You Can Go Home Again," Guest Editorial, *The Compass*, *The Metro Advertiser*, Dec. 23, 1984.

"Christmas Journey," *A Christmas Journey*, Cabbitt Productions, 2001.

"Mary," *The Atlantic Advocate*, 1980. *Shadows of the Heart*, 1998.

"The Candle in the Snow," *The Pentecostal Testimony*, Dec. 1993.

"Christmas at the Grenfell Orphanage, 1923," *Far from Home: Dr Grenfell's Little Orphan*, 2004. Flanker Press, St. John's. Reprinted 2006.

GLOSSARY

berry hocky: homemade drink from wild berries

blackjack: a jay showing grey and black

clingy: a drink made from Purity syrup

conkerbell: icicle

dribble: urinate

loo: loon

mare-browed: having eyebrows that meet in the middle

scoff: a meal

skeet: skate

squinch: screw up one's face

swanky: a drink made by mixing cranberry jam and hot water

tip: a drink, as in "a tip of moonshine"

tissing: making a hissing noise

trotter bone: the foot of certain animals eaten for food

truckling: pushing, as in truckling a toy

widdershins: a direction contrary to the sun's course, or
    counterclockwise

yoked: fitted with a yoke for carrying water buckets

NELLIE P. STROWBRIDGE is one of Newfoundland's most beloved and prolific writers. She is the winner of provincial and national awards, and has been published nationally and internationally. Her work is capsuled in The National Archives (Canada's Stamp of Approval Award), and has been studied in schools and universities as far away as Belarus.

Strowbridge, a former columnist, editorial writer and essayist, has been Writer in the Library, a mentor to young writers, and an adjudicator in the Newfoundland and Labrador Arts and Letters Awards. She has also held school workshops and hosted Gabfest for International Women's Day in Cobh, Ireland, where she was a writer-in-residence. The Canadian Embassy in Dublin also sponsored a reading and reception for her.

The author is a member of The Writers' Alliance of Newfoundland and Labrador, The Writers' Union of Canada, The League of Canadian Poets, Page One, and The Newspaper Institute of America.

Previous books: *Widdershins*, stories of a fisherman's daughter; *Doors Held Ajar* (tri-author); *Shadows of the Heart*; *Dancing on Ochre Sands* (shortlisted for the 2005 E.J. Pratt Award); and a young adult novel, *Far from Home: Dr. Grenfell's Little Orphan*.

The author lives in Pasadena with her husband, Clarence, and their boomeranging children and grandchildren.

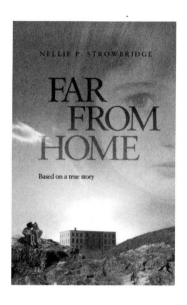

Also by Nellie P. Strowbridge

Far From Home

INSPIRED BY TRUE EVENTS

Clarissa, eleven, has been orphaned by a disease that has kept her far from home for as long as she can remember. Despite the many inmates in Dr. Grenfell's Children's Home on Newfoundland's northern tip, she lives a lonely life. Will Clarissa get to go home? If so, what will she discover about her past that will help her understand why she spent her childhood at the orphanage?

$16.95 • 5.5 x 8.5 • 227 pages • pb • ISBN-10: 1-894463-61-7

ISBN-13: 9781894463614 • Fiction • Imprint: Pennywell

The Annual Christmas Ornament Project

Outport Christmas
by Dave Hoddinott

Christmas is my favorite time of the year. One of our traditions that we like to do as a family is decorate our Christmas Tree. I have two daughters and they alternate placing the star on the treetop each year. It's always the last ornament we put on the tree. The girls then cannot wait to see the multi-colored lights on the tree.

This image "Outport Christmas" was inspired by this lighting of our Christmas Tree, which I am sure is a similar tradition with many families. The best gift of all around any Christmas Tree is a happy family.

About the Artist

David Hoddinott is a well-known landscape artist, born and raised in Newfoundland. Today, Dave lives and paints in St.John's, where he is only minutes from the ocean and countryside, which he uses as inspiration for many of his paintings. He considers Newfoundland a wonderful place to live and raise a family.

In 1995, he left his 20-year-old career in the architectural drafting and illustration field to pursue his dream of becoming a full-time artist. He works mainly in acrylics and is best known for his dramatic light-filled landscape paintings. He has been exhibiting his artwork and his paintings in-group and one-man shows since 1982. He has won several awards for his artwork and his paintings and prints are in many corporate and private collections throughout Canada, the United States and Europe.

Dave can be contacted at (709) 368-8222 or email at dave.hoddinott@nf.sympatico.ca

Distributed by

Clarenville
Area Chamber
of Commerce

Tel: (709) 466-5800   Fax: (709) 466-5803
Toll Free: 1-866-466-5800
www.clarenvilleareachamber.net
Email: info@clarenvilleareachamber.net

S ince 1999, the Clarenville Area Chamber of Commerce (CACC) has surpassed expectations of popularity and profit with the annual Christmas Ornament Project. The CACC started the Christmas Ornament project as a method to becoming self-sufficient. Since its inception, the project has become a booming success, growing each year. It has proven to be a great souvenir item for people traveling from away.

The project gives artists great exposure and it certainly adds to the preservation of our Newfoundland culture. Our product line consists of ornaments, art/greeting cards, matted art cards and limited edition prints and artist proofs. We have our products located at various retailers across the province and throughout Canada.

The product itself is a 2" x 3" pewter ornament that displays a new design from a local artist each year. The ornament is packaged with a tag, which gives information on the artist, the inspiration behind the design and a ballot to enter to win a free print.

The following is a break down of the project over the past eight years:

- 1999 -
Any Mummers Llow'd In
by Louise Colbourne Andrews

- 2000 -
Silent Night in Quidi Vidi
by Julia Bursey George

- 2001 -
Saltwater Santa
by Dawn Baker

- 2002 -
In Nan's Kitchen
by Kathy Sweetapple

- 2003 -
Kitchen Party
by Kelly McEntegart Sheppard

- 2004 -
Christmas Past with the Newfoundland Pony
by Edwin Snook

- 2005 -
Outport Christmas
by Dave Hoddinott

- 2006 -
That One!
by Troy Birmingham